# the bird factory

# the bird factory

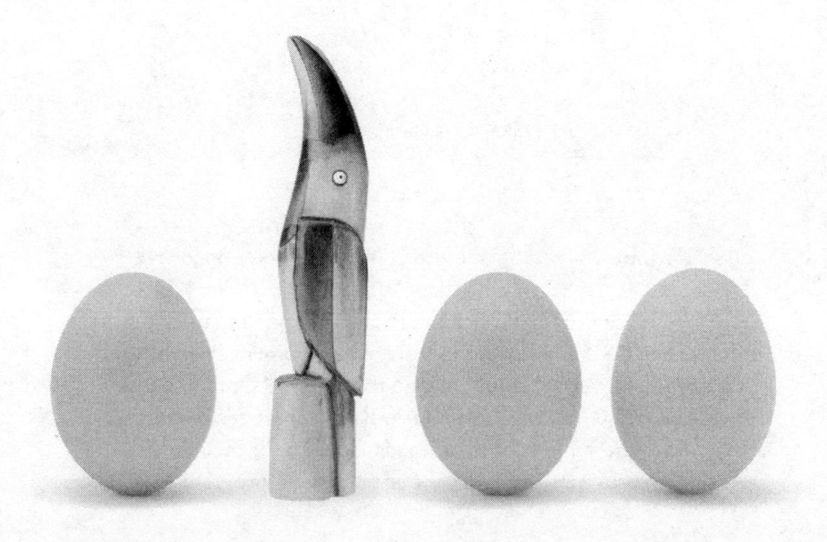

DAVID LAYTON

**Library and Archives Canada Cataloguing in Publication**

Layton, David, 1964–
The bird factory / David Layton.

ISBN 0-7710-4922-6

I. Title.

PS8623.A948B57 2005 C813'.6 C2005-900005-8

We acknowledge the financial support of the Government of Canada through the Book Publishing Industry Development Program and that of the Government of Ontario through the Ontario Media Development Corporation's Ontario Book Initiative. We further acknowledge the support of the Canada Council for the Arts and the Ontario Arts Council for our publishing program.

Typeset in Janson by M&S, Toronto
Printed and bound in Canada

This book is printed on acid-free paper that is 100% recycled, ancient-forest friendly (100% post-consumer recycled).

McClelland & Stewart Ltd.
*The Canadian Publishers*
481 University Avenue
Toronto, Ontario
M5G 2E9
www.mcclelland.com

1 2 3 4 5 09 08 07 06 05

For Annie, with love

"I hope you love birds too. It is economical.
It saves going to heaven."

— EMILY DICKINSON

the bird factory

# Empty Places

I BLAME THE RACCOONS.

They'd moved into our new home with us, using the pink, fibrous insulation of our unrenovated third-floor attic as bedding and the wooden beams as roadways. In late spring the mother produced a litter, and as we lay in bed we could hear the scampering of small feet above our heads.

Julia gave up on my promises to get rid of them and called the exterminators. Three men came to our house and after crawling around the attic for ten minutes said they wanted two thousands dollars to make it "raccoon-proof." Julia threw the men out and let the raccoons stay.

"If we're going to spend two thousand dollars, we may as well put the money toward renovating the space into a real third floor," she said.

The attic was reachable through a trap door. We climbed the narrow ladder that dropped from the ceiling in the bedroom closet and hoisted ourselves up into the empty space, careful not to disturb the raccoons, especially the mother, who we feared might attack us if she felt threatened. I swept the room with my flashlight, stopping just to one side of where Julia thought the mother and her litter might be hiding.

I suggested a guest bedroom, a den, an office.

Julia had another idea. "There might come a time when we'll want to use the upstairs space for something else." She smiled, an extra big smile because it was dark and she knew her words would make me uneasy.

"Something else?" I asked.

"We've been together four years, Luke. And we've been married for two."

"That's a pretty long time," I admitted, though it didn't feel long at all, just an eye-blink of time.

"You'd make a great father."

For a second, I thought this was why she wanted a child – so I could be a good father – but I came to my senses and recognized that this wasn't for me, but for us, for Julia.

Backing down the ladder, Julia questioned what sort of stairs we might put in. I said that unless we punched a hole in our slanted roof and put in a large dormer, the stairs would have to rise steeply, to prevent our heads from bumping into the ceiling. Another option was to put in a spiral staircase.

"So, what do you think?" asked Julia.

"I think a spiral."

"I meant about having a baby."

We were standing at the bottom of the ladder. Julia picked off loose bits of insulation that clung to my clothes and I had the weirdest impression she'd carry on until she hit bone.

"Why don't we do the third floor first, maybe get that out of the way."

"Wouldn't it be better if we co-ordinated our activities, if we did the attic *and* got pregnant all at the same time?"

"It's a suggestion," I confessed, and because one was associated with the other, I began to think of children as creatures who demanded extra space or were themselves extra space; little attics, where instead of desks and beds we'd install our longings and needs. A kind of endless renovation project.

This wasn't the best way to think about children, but at least it was a start. I hadn't thought about marriage either until Julia proposed: "It's time we got married," she'd said.

And we did. She'd slipped on my wedding ring like someone who'd had to send flowers to herself.

It wasn't that I hadn't wanted to marry Julia or that I didn't want to have children with her. It was just that I was a firm believer in not rocking the boat. Things were good. Everything was fine. I was happy, so was Julia. Why take a chance with change? Change was bad, or might be bad; it was certainly unpredictable. I'd been raised inside a rocking boat and had grown up permanently seasick. Having children might not only start the swaying again, it might tip the whole boat over. Julia, however, was an excellent swimmer, amorously embracing the water with every stroke of her arms. She said it was an illusion for anyone to think their boat could bob in exactly the same place, day after day, month after month; eventually, the current would press against you. Julia insisted that life's perpetual adversity forced you to strive toward a better future. And Julia saw a future with children.

Sex for the next few months was urgent and passionate and spontaneous. We had sex when we felt like it, and we felt like it quite a lot. Despite my concerns about children, my body seemed to possess nothing but willing confidence. Every flicker of desire was like a potential sign of success. But after six months with no results, a rising measure of fatigue and anxiety began to set in; after eight, panic. Julia began to bring home pregnancy manuals, change her foods, make sure my boxers were loose, and call out with mock lust, "It's time for servicing!" when her temperature was right.

At first we laughed because our behaviour was so much like what we imagined a desperate couple's would be. But as the months wore on, we stopped laughing – exactly when, I can't say – and our sexual trysts became increasingly mechanical. We began to sense that we were failing at the most basic human function. Our bodies were supposed to do certain things, mysterious but common enough – so why wasn't anything happening?

Julia began to spend more and more time in the bathroom. The scented swirls of bathwater, the prolonged thrum of the hair dryer, the rattling and scooping and smearing of assorted creams and oils, all failed to cover her growing apprehension.

But she tried, with clothes – evening dresses, business suits, blouses, T-shirts – heaped on hangers, jammed in drawers. She bought massive bunches of yellow flowers for her office and our home, replacing them long before they even hinted of decay. She bought a juicer and a machine that turned wheat grass into a foul-smelling drink. When she switched them on in the morning it was like waking up inside a jet-propulsion lab. I was fearful a fuse would blow.

"Do you think that's going to help?" I asked, looking at the wheat-grass machine. "You're turning into a rabbit."

"Rabbits get pregnant."

Julia took a bar-shot of the liquid, staining her mouth and teeth a florid, fecund green.

"You might think of having some yourself."

Eyeing the machine, scuffed and clogged from overuse, I took a cowardly step backward. *See, this is what I was talking about*, I thought to myself. Things were so good before; now they were not.

Julia, marking my move away from her, frowned.

"I don't care if you drink wheat grass or not," she said, though I wasn't sure if she was being entirely honest. "But you don't have to be so hostile that I'm drinking it. You make me feel like I'm the only one who's making any effort."

"That's not true."

To prove my point, I took Julia's hand and led her upstairs to the bedroom. It was a weekday; neither of us had much time before going to work. We joined our bodies in a functional embrace and, mission accomplished, I slipped back downstairs for some breakfast, coolly avoiding her machines as if they were houseguests who had overstayed their welcome. I poured some coffee from the pot and toasted some bread, still thinking about our earlier conversation. What I wanted out of life was peace and order and Julia – until now I'd thought of them as not only synonymous but inextricably linked.

I looked at the stove clock and saw it was already past nine; normally Julia would be out the door by now. It occurred to me that my departure from the bedroom had been a bit too abrupt. I walked back upstairs and found her upside down, legs buckled over the headboard, head depressed into the mattress by the weight of her body.

"Julia?"

"It's an old trick for getting pregnant." Julia's eyes, rapidly blinking past the rumpled Himalayas of our bedsheets, tracked my movements toward her. "I'm making gravity work for me. If you think about it, the human body has been poorly designed. It needs assistance."

I sat down on the edge of the bed, gently so as not to disturb her balance, and placed my hands around her ankles to help stabilize her position.

During our first year together, Julia had assiduously demanded I use a condom to prevent pregnancy as much as disease, and then for the following years she'd used a collection of devices and pills that I'd been fortunate enough not to know too much about.

"We just need more time," I said.

"I'm thirty-four. We don't have more time!"

Julia pushed back the strands of hair that had flopped over her eyes. She smiled, an upside-down smile, and then, as if suddenly remembering that her feet were pointing toward the sky, she began crying, her tears flowing backward. Nothing was going where it was supposed to.

"I want a baby."

"I know."

## 7

That evening, we listened to the raccoons. I lay in bed staring at the ceiling, hoping Julia wasn't doing the same. In our reproductive confidence we'd been fully prepared to throw out one family in order to support our own. But the raccoons were still up there and the attic was just an empty place.

"I think we need help," Julia whispered.

# Child's Play

WHEN I WAS A CHILD, Duncan, my father, built a river in our basement. There'd always been one flowing underground, he'd said. He was going to tap into it, tame it, direct it.

Water always seemed to be coming into our basement anyway. We had constant floods, and my mother took great joy in blaming Duncan for them. It had been my parents' decision to move to this neighbourhood, populated with Hungarian and Portuguese immigrants, many of whom sat on their front porches like ship stewards on deck, surveying, or so I imagined, the secret sea seeping beneath their feet; but it was Duncan who'd bought *this* house, on *this* particular street, and like all the other houses, we were slowly sinking.

Duncan, despite initial assertions that we were on terra firma, decided that we must accept our condition, embrace it even. He brought home topographical maps, hydrological surveys, city maps, present and historical, and studied them in the kitchen, while my mother, with reason, chose not to believe he'd make anything out of them. After all, she said, most people try to keep water out of the basement, not find a way to bring it in.

As for keeping our basement dry, we were fighting a losing battle. Duncan had bought us a home that, he soon found out from consultation with his maps and surveys, had been built over an active creek that sloped its way down to the lake a few miles away. And that is when he first decided to divert the flow of water into a river running through our basement.

My father was convinced it could be done. More importantly, he was convinced it *should* be done. At the kitchen table, stooped over various maps, he said to me, "This whole fucking city is floating on water!" I was about seven or eight at the time; I thought I could feel the sway of the place beneath us.

"Toronto was once a land of hills and rivers and ravines," said my father. "There were two hundred Indian villages, all these Iroquois and Mohawk portaging their way up and down in canoes. Then the settlers came and wrecked it." Duncan pulled out one of his historical bird's-eye maps, the kind that showed the shapes of important buildings, and spread it out with his palms. "Look at this. They imposed a gridiron over the ravines, flattened the whole place out."

With his fingernail as a guide, Duncan journeyed along the straight roads of the settlers' city, past the stately, noble buildings, some with flags fluttering above their peaked rooftops. I sensed I was betraying my father for finding it an orderly, proper, even beautiful place and nodded in false agreement when he said, "Just like this city to cover up the best of itself. They've turned most of the ravines into sewers."

And then there was the lake. Looking at the map, I could tell the water was the reason for the city's existence. But contrary to its early needs, the city spread up and away from the threatening shoreline, away from the cold, dark waters and wild Indians. I was thankful we lived so far from it. Now Duncan was calling up the water's untamed strength. It was a *Great* Lake, he emphasized, serviced by rivers and ravines, brooks, streams and creeks, all of them the lake's lowly but indispensable vassals. Duncan told me that if all the water from the Great Lakes escaped, Canada would be submerged under six feet of water.

Tossing aside the map, he said, "I'm going to bring the life source back out into the open."

I looked up at my father with wonder and no small amount of horror. He began to scratch his sideburns, which spread out into suburban enclaves like the city itself. I never liked it when he scratched them, which he did quite often.

One afternoon, my mother and I heard loud noises coming from the basement, and when we went downstairs to investigate, we found my father attacking the floor with a pickaxe. My mother shrieked. For no apparent reason, except perhaps for effect, Duncan had taken off his shirt. It was cold downstairs and he wasn't sweating. "It begins!" he shouted, and I ran upstairs fearful we'd all drown.

There was much to do. He had it all planned out, or so he said, though I never saw any plans, certainly nothing as proficient and detailed as the maps upstairs. He swung at the floor, breaking up the concrete, exposing the earth, the same earth that surrounded the house, only it wasn't garden earth where flowers grew – it was far darker, meaner and menacing.

Duncan dug deeper, throwing the dirt in a pile, until he reached a very large clay pipe whose presence seemed to surprise him. "That must be the sewer main," my father said. "My God, it's enormous." The idea that this clay pipe ran beneath our house filled me with alarm. My father, tugging at his sideburns, began to pace the room, formulating his course of action. "What I'm going to do is this. I'm going to dig past the pipe until we hit water. Then I'll pump the water up and let it flow along a riverbed that will run the length of the basement, then I'll drain the water into the sewer pipe, where it will continue its journey down to the lake. It's perfect."

I wondered what the purpose was of taking good fresh water and snaking it through our basement, only so it could flow directly into a sewer grate. But for all my doubts and fears, I was proud of my father. I took my friends down for tours. No one else had a father who was building a river in the basement.

Duncan liked telling me stories about sewers and rivers: in ancient Rome, he said, there was a sewer so enormous, animals slaughtered in the Coliseum could be flushed away, even elephants. "If I was a Roman I could stand over a bridge and watch animal carcasses float down the Tiber and out to sea."

I determined that when I became a man I, too, would build a river in the basement.

My mother worried. "When are you going to do some work?" she would ask Duncan, as if all that banging and excavating and planning wasn't work. But my father, whose last documentary had made enough money to buy this house, ignored her. Or rather, he failed to hear her.

My mother had her own work to do. With four cigarettes lined up at her left elbow, she sat down at her typewriter and wrote her weekly column for the *Toronto Star*, whose length was determined – or so it seemed to me – by the amount of time it took to puff away at the last ember of her last cigarette. Her face always looked a bit swollen as if her deeply held convictions had certain side effects. My mother liked to write about her cigarettes, specifically her battle to give them up. And when she found that she couldn't, my mother wrote about the miracle of vitamin C, which she'd been told by a nutritional expert could mitigate the effects of smoking. If she read a book and liked it, she'd write about it. If she saw an interesting film, she'd urge her readers to see it. And she wrote about me too. About how poorly I was doing in school and how sugar and food chemicals made me hyperactive. She thought making children sit all day behind a desk was tortuous, so she took me out of the public system and sent me to a free school. She wrote about that as well.

Emily distrusted politicians, especially American politicians, businessmen, especially American businessmen, nuclear scientists, anyone who believed in nuclear scientists, those who believed in making war, and those who made war. Especially those who made war. They resided in a special hate category and deserved one extra cigarette beside her typewriter.

I decided that I liked politicians and army generals. I was for nuclear scientists. According to my mother, these men were all engaged in unnecessary and potentially dangerous behaviour, which sounded just like my father, the man busy creating a river down in our basement.

Duncan smashed a hole in the sewer main. A foul, dank smell rose up from below. "Go upstairs and flush the toilet," my father said. "Then run back down as fast as you can."

I did as he instructed, and proudly outran the tidal surge that rushed down the pipe, on its way under the house to the lake. "This is where the river water is going to go," my father said. "Right here."

Alarmed by the smell, my mother came down to investigate and, as she'd done before, shrieked in horror when she spotted the broken pipe.

After that, my mother and I were banned from the basement for two weeks. My father built on each side of the river new concrete flooring, over which he laid down a white shag carpet, couches, and chairs. He installed pot lights and erected two small, arched bridges to span his two-foot-wide river, along with a knee-high decorative stone fence around the lip of his water hole, so no one would accidentally fall inside. Finally, he called us down.

"I'm about to let her rip!" he shouted.

My mother held a bottle of champagne by its neck, dangling it over the water hole as if she had half a mind to let it drop; I held the glasses, three of them, mine partially filled with orange juice, nervous that I'd spill and prematurely christen my father's creation.

"Let the world that is hidden from us be hidden no more!"

Duncan flipped the pump switch.

There were a few gurgles and then a narrow rivulet of water trickled over the lip of the stone fence, down a specially constructed sluice my father had decorated with Mexican tiles, and into the bending, meandering, basement riverbed itself. I handed out the glasses and dipped my finger in the now rushing water; it was surprisingly clear and made me shudder, not from the cold, but from a sense that it was unhealthy, that we'd tapped into something far worse than the sewer main that I now knew was buried only a few feet beneath me. From that moment on, we could hear the babble of running water throughout the house, greeting us for breakfast, lulling us to sleep.

You can find a picture of my parents in the newspaper archives of 1977. There they are, Duncan's wide, untamed sideburns making his face look rounder and fatter than it really was, and my mother dressed as if she were a host organism for every bright Third World fabric. There's a caption beneath the photograph. It says, innocuously: *Duncan and Emily Gray standing beside their river.*

With the river came the parties. We'd always had them – my parents liked to socialize – but now, like the river downstairs, the floodwaters of guests and wine and hashish smoke, of laughter and excited talking never seemed to recede. I didn't want all these people in our house, especially not their noises, which lingered in my ears when I was in bed trying to sleep or when I was at free school trying to take a nap on the dusty red carpet that smelled of unhappy children. There were plenty of other things to do at the free school other than take a nap, but no one made you do them, so most of us slept, pretending to think with our eyes closed, as our teachers encouraged us to do.

My walk to the free school was interrupted one morning by my father, who rolled up beside me in a borrowed pickup truck and invited me to join him on an excursion up north in search of the Canadian Shield. It was a bright, hot day so I climbed in and we drove off. When we passed the free school, Duncan shook a defiant fist at the brick-fronted building. There were kids playing outside, and it looked as if he was angry at them too. We left the city and then the suburbs and then the farm fields until there was nothing but trees and rock and lake.

It was my father's intention to find enough stone to completely cover the hole in the basement – people were getting too curious, my father said, and might trip over the low fence late at night. But as we walked along the wooded trail he spotted a small waterfall and his ambitions grew exponentially, from one of prevention to one of expansion.

We spent all afternoon hauling slabs of rocks back to the car. They were so heavy only Duncan had the strength to hoist them into the back of the truck. Pausing for rest, my father told me how everything around us had once been covered in towering ice-sheets a mile high. As they retreated from a warming world, they had scooped out the earth like fingers in pudding, leaving behind lakes and rocks; rocks that I was helping my father carry.

My father's idea was this: he would mount pieces of Canadian Shield against the back wall of the basement, layer them like roofing tile, and direct the water to run over them. He was going to build a waterfall.

I knew we were disturbing something that should otherwise have been left alone, something that might harm us. I learned then it is best to leave things as they are.

The waterfall brought even more people to our home, as I feared it would. They came to see the waterfall, but stayed for the company, which included people from places like New

York, San Francisco, London, Rome. Now people arrived for a party and remained behind, sometimes for days, sleeping in the spare bedroom or on the couch in the basement where they'd be lulled to sleep by the cascading water.

I wanted to put a lock on my door; strangers opened it to inquire after the bathroom and one night, for no accountable reason, a woman entered my room, shut the door, wept disconsolately, wiped away her tears, and then walked out. Before she left, the woman looked at me with an expression of intimate gratitude, as if I'd helped her overcome her sadness.

I sensed danger and tried to warn my mother. I felt something had to be said and that my father would never listen to me. My mother, I knew, had her doubts about the river and the waterfall, though she'd become surprisingly amenable to their existence. I tried to impress upon her that things were getting out of control, but she was caught up in her own projects and, rather than listen, she tried to drag me into them too. She took me to what she thought were worthy demonstrations, even if they fell on school days, because, in her opinion, it was good for me to be exposed – as if it were a disease – to a world wider than my own. In the end, my warnings were lost among the chanting demands of equal rights and justice for all.

It was after one of these rallies that my mother and I returned and heard a loud, repetitive banging coming from the basement. Thinking there was something wrong with the pump, we went down to investigate and found my father, naked, pressed up against a woman in the waterfall.

That was the first time she left us.

# Bad News

DR. HENDERSON CLASPED HIS HANDS behind his head, leaned back in his chair, and offered us a smile that, like his desk, was oversized and broken-in from countless encounters with patients like Julia and me.

I knew – because Julia had told me – just how lucky we were to be at the Centre for Reproductive Technology. Our doctor was considered to be the best and therefore the most difficult to get an appointment with. He typically had an eight-month waiting list; we'd waited only six weeks.

This was Julia's doing. She was the master of crisis, a woman who made a career of it, and she'd applied her skills of industry and persuasion to get us through the front door in ways I could not explain but had learned to accept.

Crisis Management – that's what my wife did. There wasn't a case of financial mismanagement, sexual impropriety, an outbreak of food poisoning, or an oil spill that Julia couldn't find a way to manage. With experience like hers, there was no way Julia would have to wait eight months for an appointment, or settle for the second-best doctor.

Dr. Henderson picked up our file.

"Julia Riddell, thirty-four, according to the tests no scarring on the Fallopian tubes, regular periods, no medical history worth mentioning."

Satisfied, he turned his attention to me. A week ago, I'd handed over a sample of my sperm for inspection; now it was time for the results.

"Luke Gray, thirty-five, a quantity of your sperm is malformed. The tails are crooked, too short. They swim in circles." The doctor twirled his index finger. "Of course, to be successful, they need to swim straight."

Reluctantly, I looked down at my lap. *You idiots.*

Leading up to this appointment, Julia and I had redoubled our sexual efforts in the creeping, somewhat creepy, almost magical belief that only now, with an eminent fertility specialist awaiting us, would we conceive. But children – my children – would not arrive by way of a darkened night, but by the bright lights of Dr. Henderson's office.

"Let me just say that I have patients with far lower counts. Sometimes, and in some conditions, there is simply no viable sperm whatsoever, or so few that we must inject them directly into the ovum." Dr. Henderson squeezed thumb and forefinger together and stabbed at the air above him. "Put in layman's terms, you have lazy sperm."

Julia reached for my hand. "Lazy? Is that a proper diagnosis?"

Ignoring Julia's question, Dr. Henderson continued.

"Have you ever had any communicable diseases?" The doctor looked at me with that distinct, intense blankness that comes from asking rude and intrusive questions hourly. "Syphilis? Gonorrhea? Chlamydia?"

"Yes."

"Which one?"

I offered a disconsolate shrug. Could I be expected to appraise the sting and drip of each infection?

"You mean you don't know?"

"Should I?"

"Yes, as a matter of fact."

Julia, pert and attentive and perhaps feeling that any evasion was a hindrance to success, shouted out, "He has herpes!" and looked at me as if she had just won a contest and should be awarded a ribbon.

Armed with information, Dr. Henderson scribbled my condition down on a piece of paper. "Do you smoke?" he asked.

"Yes, he smokes," Julia answered with a look of aggressive concern.

"You need to stop. Immediately."

"Why?" Julia asked, alarmed.

"Because it's a primary cause of infertility."

Dr. Henderson scratched his head and involuntarily I did the same. I was mimicking him, following him, hating him.

"I don't believe you," I said.

The doctor laughed.

"Well, you don't have to take my word for it, look at the studies. Fact, cigarettes cause damage on the genetic level. Fact, a flap is produced over the head of the sperm."

Dr. Henderson made a fist with one hand, wrapped his other around it, and, as if it were a boa constrictor, squeezed.

"There's no way for the sperm to penetrate the egg."

"Like uncircumcised sperm," Julia added helpfully, but again the doctor had the good sense to ignore her.

"Furthermore," he continued, "I've put my mouth where my cigarette once was, so to speak. I smoked over a pack a day for more than fifteen years. After six months of not smoking, my wife became pregnant."

Dr. Henderson exposed his teeth from a chubby, winterized face, flushed from a lack of exercise and an overheated room. It was a smile of sorts; a victorious one. He glanced at a gold-framed photograph that he had no doubt proudly positioned on his desk.

"Those are my three children," he stated.

"They're beautiful." Julia stared at the picture with admiring eyes.

Littering Dr. Henderson's desk, like trophies, were photos of other children beside his own, baby pictures delivered to him by former patients. One was signed, "Noah, our little bundle of joy!" Another simply had a "Thank You" scrawled excitedly across its bottom. These pictures were meant to attest to Dr. Henderson's potency, I supposed, and make us, his new patients, feel that under his supervision, success was imminent, that we too would be sending him a picture. I found them cruel.

Dr. Henderson looked at us with professional concern. "I know this is difficult. We have several psychiatrists on call here at the clinic. I won't kid you. This can be a very trying time."

Julia breathed in a precise amount of air and looked steadily at Dr. Henderson. She was ready. In the car, on our way over here, she'd unclasped her blonde hair and let it run straight down her back without any pins or clips to dam up and reroute the flow. For Julia, there could be no diversions. Not now.

"We'll start with a prescription of folic acid for Luke, which should increase potency. And when we collect his sperm, we'll give it a wash before insemination."

"Wash?" I queried.

"A sperm wash. Centrifugal force. We spin the sperm around and remove the unwanted ones, the ones with the deformed tails and so forth. They just get in the way. What your wife receives, when we inseminate her, is the best there is, the *crème de la crème*." He chuckled.

Dr. Henderson's office inhabited a corner suite on the nineteenth floor of a tall building downtown. In the tower next to his, I could clearly see a man in another office dialling a number on his telephone. For an instant I thought that Dr. Henderson's phone would ring and it would be the man behind the window.

"Do you travel a lot for your job?" the doctor asked me.

"Not really."

"Under 'Occupation,' you state that you're a business owner. What line of business are you in?"

"I make mobile birds."

Dr. Henderson blinked with incomprehension.

"They're beautiful," Julia said.

Apparently everything today was beautiful. His children, my birds, everything.

"And you," he asked, turning to Julia, "do you travel a lot?"

"Yes," she nodded. "I do."

"You'll have to co-ordinate your schedule with my office. We'll need to monitor your eggs for size and production. There's a drug regime. I suggest you pay for everything here with a credit card that gives you frequent-flyer points, that way you can take a nice trip somewhere," the doctor said, and in the back of my mind I registered my resentment that he'd said this to Julia and not to me.

Dr. Henderson picked up a pencil and drew an outline of a uterus, with double lines on either side indicating the Fallopian tubes with two imperfect circles dangling at each end: Julia's ovaries.

"Think of me as the conductor and you as the talented musicians." With the tip of his pencil, he stabbed Julia's graphite ovaries, the musical notes, the score, from which he, Dr. Henderson, would conduct his symphony.

Then he closed our file and bid us goodbye, though not before handing me a prescription for folic acid.

He was a hateful man. As we exited the doctor's office I saw that Julia had gone pale, save for a touch of red around her ears, as if what she'd heard this morning embarrassed her.

"How are you feeling?" I asked as we walked past the waiting room, which was filled with women like Julia, many of them sitting alone.

"Optimistic," she said, surprising me. "That didn't go too badly."

I thought it had gone terribly and wondered if it was possible that optimism fiercely pursued led to a certain madness.

Julia pushed the button for the elevator.

The clinic's offices were situated inside one of the few structures from the 1970s Brutalist style that had retained its prestige. While my father had built a river in his basement, others had thrown up buildings like these – buildings of brushed concrete, flat roofs, and high-speed elevators that would one day whisk infertile couples to and from their appointments. Julia's parents, on the other hand, had carried on with their lives in stubborn ignorance of the mad diggers and untalented builders. The Riddells had bought a house in staid North Toronto shortly after Julia's birth, and had remained in the area ever since, living a controlled, rigid existence and enrolling their daughter into Havergal, a private girls' school, where she had excelled in smoking dope and getting straight As. They would never have expected their daughter, whom they'd primed for success, to meet with this sort of obstacle.

"Just wondering," said Julia, "but *do* you know the difference between syphilis, gonorrhea, and chlamydia?"

"I don't. And no one else does either."

"How about Dr. Henderson?"

"The great conductor? He's a joke. Did you get a look at those photographs on his desk? All those babies, like they were his."

Julia became defensive. "I didn't see anything wrong with them."

"Are you telling me that you'd let him mount a picture of our baby on his desk?" *Staring out at desperate, wannabe parents like us?*

Julia didn't answer. She stepped into the elevator and we drifted downwards, stopping at several floors to admit the sort of well-turned-out people Julia's parents might have expected their daughter to marry. While I couldn't say exactly what the men did for a living, I was fairly certain it didn't include making mobile birds. They probably had higher sperm counts too.

When we reached the lobby, Julia slipped into one of the revolving doors leading outside. Office workers, some in small groups, others alone, were smoking cigarettes under the shadow of the hulking building. I automatically reached for the pack in my front pocket.

Hailing a cab, Julia said, "You heard what the doctor said about smoking. If you ever needed a good excuse to stop, now you have one." Without a goodbye, she drove away.

I was glad to see her go. *Let her rush back to work*, I thought. Let her attend more lucrative crises, ones that were more readily solvable.

# If Anyone Has a Reason Why

THE BIRDS BROUGHT JULIA TO ME. She'd spotted them in a store while searching for a present and had followed them back to the small downtown studio where they'd been born. I worked alone in those days, in six-hundred square feet of industrial space. I was cutting bird wings with a jigsaw when I saw her through the plastic fog of my goggles, weaving unsteadily toward me. My immediate thought was that she was drunk until I realized she was trying to avoid the splatters of paint on the floor. Then she took her shoes off – high-heeled pumps – and laughed, because she was surrounded by dozens of birds dangling down from the ceiling, jumbo-sized seagulls up top, smaller birds below, all with their balanced wings stretched out in flight.

"It's like walking into the sky," she'd said.

What did I see in Julia? Everything. There she was bobbing and weaving, looking as if she were off balance, which is just the sort of thing I would think about people, when in fact she was charting a course through the obstacles in her way.

Her hair was short then, the length cut off at the neck in the defiant fashion, I reflected, of someone who'd just ended a relationship, of someone who wanted to chop off the past and sweep it away. Julia surveyed the room, the birds, the dirty windowpanes, me. She had a way of steadfastly fixing her hazel eyes on objects that interested her. *I* interested her.

"I saw your seagulls in a store and came to ask if you would make a stork for me. I have a friend who's pregnant."

"I've never made a stork before," I said.

"Then this will be your first."

Julia reached for the only chair in the room and sat down as if I was going to make her bird right there and then. It was raining outside, just a light drizzle, but the wind, which was strong, made it sound worse than it was. I poured us both some tea, embarrassed by the stains on the inside of the cups. With no one but myself to impress, I'd obviously let things go.

"It feels so sheltered in here," she said. "Isolated. Like an uninhabited island."

"Not entirely uninhabited," I pointed out.

She gave me a warm smile. "How long have you been doing this?"

*Forever*, I thought. "A few years," I said.

"Do you work alone?"

"Yes."

"Don't you get lonely?"

"No."

"I would."

Troubled by what she'd said, I sipped my tea. Who was this person to come in here and ask me about being lonely? "Do you always ask strangers such personal questions?"

"It depends on the stranger," she answered, and something in the way she said it made me less defensive. "Will you make me a stork?"

Storks are wading birds, a scourge of snakes. They stand in the shallows on one leg, patiently waiting to grab a meal with their long beaks. And like most birds, storks have an expression of nervous intemperance, but I wouldn't have sold many birds if I made them look as they did in real life, like they were about to pluck your eyes out, or attack the first quiver of a child's curious fingers.

"I'll try," I said.

Julia looked at her watch. "It's almost lunchtime. Are you hungry? I could get us something to eat and bring it back here. We could have a picnic."

*A picnic?*

Julia slipped her shoes back on. "I won't be long." She left without asking what I'd like.

During her absence, I cleared off a section of the worktable that ran along two walls of the factory. Duncan, utilizing the carpentry skills he'd acquired long ago in the basement, had fixed bracings to the wall so that the table was legless, leaving room for storage and machinery underneath. Wiping the section of table clean, I was reminded of those first birds I'd made after the river had dried up. Maybe Julia was right. *I am lonely*, I thought. *And I've always been lonely.*

Julia returned with bags of food. "I've brought some wine." She pulled the bottle out of its paper sleeve and presented it to me for inspection. "And some cheese and olives." She ignored the space I'd made for us on the worktable and walked to the middle of the room, dragging behind her the floor canvas I used to catch the dripping paint. She turned it over and spread it out like a bedsheet.

"Let's eat here."

Julia laid out bright blue paper plates, canary-yellow napkins, and two surprisingly elegant wineglasses.

"Cheers," I said, somewhat dazed, raising my glass to Julia and to the birds above us.

Julia, looking around her again, said, "This is your business, isn't it?"

"Who else would want it?" I joked.

"I wish I had the guts to go out on my own. I work as a crisis-management consultant for a firm that seems more interested in its own crises than in anyone else's. Have you ever worked for a large company? It's all pointless meetings, politics, and fear." Julia, who'd taken her shoes off again, wiggled her toes. "When you work for someone else, you're never in control. There's always someone with power over you. That's the worst of it, at least for someone like me. Sometimes I feel so exhausted I could cry." Julia took another sip of wine. "I usually don't talk like this on the first date."

"This is a date?"

"Relax," she said, "it's a picnic."

A pungent, oily smell of past industrial strength still clung to the brick walls of the six-storey warehouse. It was a strange place for a picnic, I thought. Stranger still for a date. I was not a dater. I did not go out on dates. Six months ago, I'd slept with the woman who designed Web pages two floors below me. On the floor above, I'd slept with the woman who made life-sized dolls. That was two months ago. I no longer spoke to either of them.

Each of the floors was accessed by a wooden freight elevator that creaked out its complaint whenever service was demanded of it; I heard its groan as Julia sipped her wine, as if in despair at the modern occupants who no longer manufactured the masculine machines of days past. Every time I stepped inside and closed the gate, I felt like an inadequate gift dropped inside the wrong package. Because, when you got right down to it, what sort of man made mobile birds for a living?

Julia reached up and tapped one of the birds, setting its wings fluttering.

What was this woman doing here in all this mess? But there was no mess where we sat. Just a patch of comfort and order that had never existed before. And when Julia turned away from the birds and leaned over to kiss me I thought she might be the person who could bring the same comfort and order into my own life.

The stork I made for Julia had a regal friendliness, with widespread wings, gently curved as if skimming above placid waters. I bought a small plastic baby, swaddled it in cloth, and attached it to the stork's snake-eating beak with an oversized safety pin.

I brought the bird to Mia's party. Mia was Julia's pregnant friend, who, when she answered the door, squealed in excitement and led us upstairs to the baby room, already kitted out with bedding and shelves and comforting night lights.

"That's where we'll put it," Mia said to us, pointing to an empty patch of ceiling above the expectant crib. Mia was barely showing. *She can't be more than four months*, I thought, suddenly feeling that the room was too small and cloying and obsessively female. There was already the scent of baby in the room, of lotion, talcum powder, and burp. I began edging toward the door until she finally released us with a promise of drinks and we gratefully joined the rest of the party downstairs.

I hadn't seen Julia since our kiss at the bird factory, though we'd spoken on the phone. I didn't particularly want to go to a baby shower for our first official date, but I did want Julia, so I feigned enthusiasm when she suggested it and offered to pick her up at eight. She was waiting for me outside her apartment when I arrived and I noticed she'd dressed herself up. I don't know why I'd found this so touching, or surprising, but I did. I'd done my best to look presentable but, as always, I'd held something back – I'd neglected to rub my shoes with the foam brush that made them shine, or wear my crispest, sharpest shirt, or shave with extra diligence – that way I wasn't tempting the gods, I wasn't going out on a limb just to fall the full distance when things didn't work out.

I went home with her that night.

And I never really left. Julia said that, as a matter of policy, she generally didn't ask men to move in after a month, but there was no point paying rent on my apartment when hers would do just fine.

Living with Julia happened naturally, effortlessly, as if men and women had been designed to purposely, fruitfully share themselves in close confines. This had not occurred to me before.

We developed a routine. We'd wake up together in the morning and I'd gently peel back the covers so I could see Julia's resting body, still coiled and vulnerable; then I'd get out of bed to make us coffee while Julia suited up like a soldier preparing for battle. She'd eat two slices of toast with honey, drink the coffee I'd poured into her favourite blue mug, then march off to manage and dissipate all the minor crises of the world.

Julia's apartment had co-ordinated furniture in the living room and a supply of fluffy towels folded and stacked in the hall closet. It had a spare bedroom where visiting guests could tuck themselves into crisp sheets. The guest room was like Mia's baby room; it mostly sat empty and waiting but it was there, like a luxury item.

Julia treated the apartment itself like one large guest room, a place to visit, rather than a home. The first time I'd been by myself, wondering what liberties a man who'd just slept with its occupant could take, I'd peered into the kitchen cabinets, my heart beating just a bit faster because looking at someone's food and pot storage area was, I believed, somewhat of a violation. Sets of dishes were stacked with the lonely precision of someone who rarely used them. There were a dozen tall blue glasses (four rows, three to a row) and a dozen shorter blue glasses, separated, like families of the bride and the groom, into different halves of the shelf. There was an expensive pepper grinder with no pepper in it. It was the kitchen of a person who worked a lot.

I spent a fair amount of time by myself in Julia's apartment, which quickly became my apartment too because Julia was away at work so much. The exhaustion she spoke of when we'd first met became understandable when I saw the hours she put in.

"I work a lot less now than I did before," she said.

"Before" was before me, when she had lived with a man she did not love. He'd asked her to marry him and she'd accepted.

"He was very successful," Julia said by way of explanation. "I realized just in time that that's what I'd been trained to look for in a husband. It still shocks me to realize how easy it is to marry someone you don't love. In fact, I think it might be easier because emotions don't get in the way."

Julia told me this shortly after I'd moved the last of my meagre possessions worthy of transport into the apartment – a chair, one bedroom lamp, a brass soap container Julia took a fancy to, and one seagull. What I brought pleased her inordinately. I sometimes complimented myself that my few pieces of furniture liberated the perfect, impersonal order Julia had imposed upon her apartment. Their inadequacies – my own as well, I supposed – made Julia linger over her morning coffee and brought her home at night from work.

"I admire you," she told me, and when I asked her why, she said it was because I knew just how much of any one thing I needed. "Everybody I know is always fighting for more of what they already have. I was taught to never be happy with what I had. If I got a B+ in school I was supposed to get an A, if I am a director I need to become a vice-president. It never ends. But you don't seem to care about any of that, about other people's judgment. You run your own business doing what you like. You don't answer to anyone. You're autonomous. You're free."

It was nonsense, what Julia was saying. I'd never been free. I certainly wasn't autonomous or clear of judgment. Any thoughts to the contrary were quickly extinguished by the creaking elevator that moaned out its complaint whenever I came to make my birds. The birds hadn't made me free, as Julia thought. They'd imprisoned me.

And as for Julia's friends, despite my first impression of Mia, whenever she and her husband, Roger, would come over for dinner, bringing a well-reviewed bottle of wine, I was struck by how incredibly sensible they appeared: Roger worked in computers, Mia as an account executive for a mutual-fund company. Despite the baby growing inside of her, Mia said she planned to work right up to the last month of her pregnancy. And they'd already chosen the daycare for when Mia would go back. They talked about the world as if it could never harm them, and for laughs I'd tell them of my father and his river in the basement where the dead 1970s flowed past.

There I was, just recently embarking upon my thirties, unable to believe my luck. I thought, despite my birds, I'd finally walked off that rotting, swaying rowboat I'd been floating on for all those years and traded it in for a gleaming white cruise ship, the kind with fiesta decks and rock-climbing walls and equipped, high above the bridge, with a twirling radar that constantly swept the world's oceans for pockets of bad weather.

# Seagulls

THAT FIRST NIGHT, and in the following days that my mother stayed away, Duncan and I ate the food in the fridge and then, when that was gone, went out shopping and bought prepared foods that looked more like gifts than meals.

In my mother's absence, the house went silent, as if it was displeased with us. The basement door, previously left open, was closed and I was forced to go downstairs if I wanted to hear the sound of the river water, which I found soothing, but which I also knew was the source of all our problems.

Duncan spent most of his time sleeping down there, his body contorted in one of the basement chairs, one hand reaching for a sideburn like an orangutan clinging to a branch. There was a couch, but he never used it – I had the impression my father wished to punish himself – so I slept on it instead, often falling asleep with my arms crossed over my body, just like Duncan.

My mother had been a quick leaver, packing her bags seemingly in minutes, walking out to the curb before the cab had arrived to take her away. Her departure had been conducted with a minimum of noise: I remember only the hushed skirting of dresses and pants being taken out of their closet. She hadn't said a word to me, or to Duncan; she'd just left. Later, I found a note on my bed, leaning up against the pillow, printed in block letters so I wouldn't have to ask my father to decipher her tight handwriting. Although she had to go away for a while, she wrote, she loved me and wanted me to know that her absence had nothing to do with me, which, when I lay on the couch beside Duncan, listening to the river, seemed like a lie. Everything my mother did had to do with me.

"When is she coming back?"

"Soon."

"When?"

"When soon is over."

I didn't calculate how long she stayed away because counting made it feel longer, but I remember how tanned her skin looked the day she returned, the tropical smell of it too. It was so unlike our own unnatural pallor as we lay sleeping in the basement, Duncan on his chair, me on the couch, my mother bronzed like a giant scoop of caramel ice cream, standing on the opposite side of the riverbank.

"What are you *doing*, Duncan?"

"I'm sleeping, that's what I'm doing."

"It's ten o'clock in the morning!"

Duncan, looking momentarily rattled by my mother's appearance, closed his eyes against her.

"It's a school day," she said. "Luke needs to go to school. And you need to get up, stop playing in the water, and start working on another film. Otherwise I won't stay."

"I want an open marriage."

"That's your answer?"

"Everybody has one."

"Has what?"

"An open marriage."

"Who? Who has one?"

Duncan came up with a few names, all of them challenged by my mother as being nothing of the kind.

"Why should we be like everybody else?" Duncan said, switching tactics.

My father's belligerence confused me. We'd not done well without my mother, and it struck me as being in our best interests to make sure we'd never have to again. He couldn't sleep down here permanently, I thought, and he couldn't expect me to either.

"Is the marriage open for both of us, Duncan? Is that what you want, both of us crawling out the window at night?"

"You can go out the front door if you like."

"Then that's exactly what I'll do," my mother said, reaching out across the river for my hand.

I was reluctant to offer it. As glad as I was to see her, she'd left me behind and hadn't called; if she wanted me she would have to fight harder.

"C'mon, I'm taking you to school."

"No."

"You have to go."

I shook my head stubbornly.

"Go on," my father said, pleased to display his authority over me. "Your mother's right, you need to go to class."

My teachers, who hadn't seen me since my mother had left the house, were surprised and welcoming, if seemingly unconcerned by my long absence. I spent the day wandering around quietly from room to room, expecting to find another note on my bed when I returned home after school. During my wanderings, nobody ordered me to do anything; nobody expected me to do anything. There were no walls, few rules, and everything was just what my father would have wanted for himself: free schools were like open marriages for children.

It seemed that over the course of the day my mother had decided on her revenge. She picked me up and, to my surprise, led us back home, calling out for Duncan to carry her newly purchased IBM typewriter from the car. In reply to Duncan's request for an open marriage, she had decided to work as hard as she could, with the expectation that he would feel guilty and work even harder. She would force him to have a purpose, whether he wished to have one or not.

The new typewriter was a source of great wonder. It had a single ball, and upon this unitary sphere were all the letters of the alphabet and all the numbers too and other things like brackets and dollar signs and exclamation marks. Lying in bed at night I would attempt to calculate the seemingly endless permutations, but always fell asleep before finding an answer that I could carry with me throughout the day.

Duncan might have wanted to find an answer as well, but for different reasons, because he heard, as I did, the IBM ball, the jump and punch of it, and knew that every keystroke was a body blow directed at him. He'd taken to hiding in his office, but he couldn't block out the low, rattling hum of the electric machine, nor stop my mother from opening the sliding doors of his office without knocking.

I would spot my father sitting behind the massive mahogany desk he'd purchased from a bankruptcy auction, looking futile and immensely unproductive.

"Can't you see I'm busy!" he'd yell at my mother.

Looming above him was the poster to his last film, *Sweet Surrender*, which my mother had tacked up on the wall several years earlier. Before the river was built, my mother had liked to go down to the basement and watch his film, the images flickering on the portable movie screen, cast from our two-reel projector. It was a documentary about a commune in the deserts of Arizona. Its fair-haired leader, a man with double-jointed fingers and an alarming sense of his own certainty, talked a lot about the sharing of communal land, food, women, and children, the latter fathered by himself and those few he anointed. There were long silences, which my father filled with desert noise – wind and insects.

I sometimes joined my mother in the basement, never for very long, but often enough that I'd seen most of the film, particularly the parts about the children who were simultaneously neglected and cosseted by adults who bickered in passive, low voices. It seemed a dangerous place, bound to fail in a potentially dangerous way, and Duncan filmed it all so lovingly and carefully that I remember thinking how sorry he must have felt for these people, who he knew were doomed.

So now, while my father sat brooding under his poster, my mother perfected her typing, writing articles about every imaginable subject except the one that really mattered to all of us: open marriages. I never heard Duncan or my mother ever speak directly of it again, but the river still flowed as a reminder – beneath my father's hunched back as he began to gather his notes and papers like a small boy chasing his own bubbles; beneath my mother as she assaulted another virgin strip of paper with her IBM ball; beneath my fearful anxiety that my father's eyes might linger, even for a second, on an attractive model on television or a woman on the street. I became suspicious of all the married guests who came to our house – they might have open marriages too. Nobody felt safe; anything could happen.

As it turned out, my anxieties were justified. Duncan never again slept with a woman in the waterfall – he did it somewhere else. And when he was caught he would silently carry my mother's bags down the landing and out to the waiting taxi like an overaged bellhop. My mother always shielded her eyes from me and hurried out the door. When the taxi sped away, Duncan would walk back to the house, aggrieved, as if he hadn't been given a sufficient tip for his troubles.

Duncan told me my mother was having a hard time understanding the new possibilities opening up in his life. Her pain was understandable and deeply regrettable, he said, but in this crowded world if you took so much as one step forward, you were bound to tread on someone else's toes, in this case my mother's. It was wrong, he said, to let other people's pain take possession of you. That way led to guilt and unhappiness.

It was around the third time my mother left that she snuck back and fetched me one morning, just after sunrise, and told me we were off on a trip. Duncan, unusual for him, was sleeping in the bedroom, and as we crept past, I saw his sprawled, naked body, sheets pushed away, looking very unlike a man who was stepping on anyone's toes but his own. My mother looked at him with pity and rage.

We got into the car and I felt something like joy. My mother was taking me with her. We drove along the north side of Lake Ontario, past the steel mills of Hamilton, over the humped and high bridge that spans the narrowing end of the lake, from north to south. We entered America. I thought we were going to visit Niagara Falls, where all that water my father talked about, including the water from our very own basement, could be seen sweeping over the edge of one lake and dropping into the basin of another. Instead, we took a bend in the road and followed the signs to a place called Love Canal.

We pulled up to the edge of a crowd full of noisy, shouting people. My mother told me to get out and, after rummaging in the trunk, handed me a sign that said: "KIDS ARE STILL BEING POISONED." I looked blankly at the sign and then at my mother, who nodded at me with encouragement. The land beneath us was polluted, she explained. A company had dumped its industrial waste into the earth, into a canal, and it had resurfaced. Now the people who lived here wanted to leave. We were here to help them.

*This is our trip?* I thought. *This is why my mother came back for me?*

I threw the sign on the ground and demanded to know why my mother had brought me here. I didn't want any part in helping anyone that day. I started to cry.

"Luke, I want you to grow up to be the sort of person who helps others. You can't always think about yourself."

But I wasn't thinking about myself. I wanted *her* to think about me.

"I want to go home!" I yelled.

"Soon," my mother said, "soon."

A fence ran between the good land and the bad land. Just a common fence, like the kind I'd seen in Toronto, bordering schools and warehouses and parks. My mother and all the other protesters stood on one side of the fence, the good side, and pointed their placards toward the other side, the bad side, as if the bad just stopped, in a straight, easy line.

I wanted to leave immediately, but my mother was too busy saving the world. While I waited, miserable and alone, I saw birds sailing in the sky above, tilting their wings, changing course, landing on the good side and the bad side, ignoring the fence and the protesters and me. Watching them, I began to imagine they were like flying sponges, soaking up spots of pollution every time they set foot on the ground, taking it up with them into the open, empty sky.

We didn't return to the house after the protest; instead we drove back to Toronto and stayed with friends of my mother. She took me out of the free school – perhaps because, like me, she equated free schools with open marriages and Duncan's own unwieldy desires – and placed me in a proper classroom with desks I found impossible to remain seated in. I suddenly had what I'd craved – rules and lessons and discipline – but part of me had become used to the way things had been and I felt polluted, by Love Canal, by the river, and I knew that no fence, no boundary could stop the seepage from one side of me to the other.

My mother had been polluted as well. Within weeks of our return from Love Canal we moved back in with Duncan, returning without fanfare or announcement. The first night, we all had dinner together like nothing had happened. My mother and father somehow managed to get along, to pass the potatoes and even to laugh once in a while though no one, so far as I could tell, said anything particularly humorous. I was glad we were all back together – it was better than being alone with Duncan in the basement, or with my mother in someone else's house – but I was aware that she shouldn't have returned, that she shouldn't have given in so easily. My parents' marriage was a mystery to me. It was as if they each had an abiding need to confuse and humiliate themselves in front of the other. I blamed the river for this. Its poison leached up from below into our feet, minute after minute, day after day, on its way to tumble over the Falls and settle in Love Canal.

The next few months passed without incident until news of the Jonestown massacre broke. Suddenly my father's decision to go off and film an obscure cult in Arizona in the early '70s was considered an act of great prescience. Everyone wanted to know about cults, how they worked, who joined them and why. I pretended, for the experiment of it, that my father's disembodied voice on radio interviews belonged to a complete stranger. I asked myself if I could believe that this was the voice of a man who slept in a chair in the basement with a river flowing past him. He didn't sound like that person at all.

After Jonestown, Duncan abandoned the river and the basement and re-emerged with an almost manic self-confidence. After years of lethargy, my father threw himself into making a new film. He began collecting strange wooden masks and spears and feathers, which he liked to point to while telling me that everyone on the planet was linked by common myths. "Take the flood," he said. "Every culture has a myth about the great flood. But we live in a world without myths! We live without dreams and people who don't dream go insane!"

If anyone was going insane, it was my father. It was the river all over again, but since Duncan was making a film instead of breaking apart the basement, my mother believed progress was being made.

Duncan began to disappear from the house for days at a time, and I found that I missed him. When I asked my mother where he was, she told me he was out working, and the way she said it implied we should be happy he was busy.

It seemed that Duncan worked right up until the day a limousine, which Duncan had ordered in celebration, arrived to take us to the screening. We sat close to the front, in the middle seats, and watched *Angry Voices*, a documentary about Haitian voodoo, Rio breasts, the hajj, West African fertility ceremonies, and other assorted cults and carnivals. To offer parallels and context, Duncan inserted clips of rock concerts that even then must have seemed dated.

"The West," said the narrator's voice, "has lost its faith in faith." The voice belonged to my father.

I saw my mother place a victorious hand over Duncan's, patting and rubbing it like she did when we used to sit in the basement and watch *Sweet Surrender*. She revelled in the experience of watching Duncan's new film, and it was only then that I began to understand how much my mother loved him; she must have known – she was too smart not to – that his film was deplorable.

And we weren't the only ones who knew. My father, despite his faults, was not a stupid man: *he* knew that he'd made a poor film, an embarrassing, dumb, outdated film, he just couldn't bring himself to admit that it wasn't Emily's fault.

My father came to believe that if he hadn't had to console my mother, if he hadn't needed to win her back, he wouldn't have made that film. The film and my mother became linked in his mind and in consequence the very thing that was intended to bring peace into our household brought nothing but further dissent and animosity.

Duncan refused to make another documentary.

My mother, who knew how bad his latest film had been but still believed in him, in his talents, pleaded with him until she realized that he wasn't going to change his mind. "Why don't you teach?" she finally suggested.

"Because I don't want to."

"You have to do *something*."

"You didn't come back to me to nag me all day, did you? And why do I have to do anything? Why must we all *do* something?"

"Because we need the money. Because otherwise we become restless and bored and do stupid things. Besides, I think you'd make a terrific teacher. You'd like it."

My mother was worried. She feared he would start another project like the river, not knowing, as I did, that *Angry Voices* was simply its continuation. "We don't know what he's capable of," she told me one day, without a touch of irony or humour, and she was right, we didn't.

Duncan, like a stubborn child, said he didn't want to teach, that he'd be lousy at it. He must have believed teaching would be the end of him, an admission, most hurtfully from his own wife, that his career was over.

He took refuge in the basement – he'd abandoned his office upstairs – and sat there in his chair, for hours at a time, sleeping mostly, an open book splayed across his stomach. When he eventually ascended he did so with his hands in his pockets, as if he'd been out for a long stroll.

It seemed to me that all of our problems had begun with the river, that my early sense of foreboding had been right. As long as the river flowed in our basement, I reasoned, we would never be happy. We needed to be evacuated, like the people in Love Canal, but I knew we were stuck here. I found myself thinking about the birds, the way they flew above all the good and the bad, and I envied them. I longed for their freedom.

With that idea in my mind I snuck down to the basement one afternoon. On a shelf in the furnace room above the pickaxe, its metal tips still flecked with pieces of stone floor, rested my father's hand tools. It was with these tools and an old piece of wood that I made my first bird.

It didn't look like much of a bird. I'd cut out the body using a handsaw and didn't as yet have an idea of what kind of bird I wanted to carve, I'd just thought *bird*. But over time, I came closer to what I'd seen at Love Canal – I painted their underbellies white, carved out strong, lean ocean wings and necks. Each began, slowly, to take the shape of a seagull.

Duncan, so adamant against my mother's suggestion of teaching, carefully taught me how to drill two holes in the upper part of the bird body and two corresponding holes in the wings so that I could tie them together rather than glue the wings on top. He recommended plywood for the wings and explained the difference between hardwoods and softwoods and, experimenting himself, showed me how to string the birds up so that they could hang down from the ceiling. It was my father who made my birds fly.

After school, I worked on my birds in an area in the furnace room I'd cleared for myself. From his chair across the river my father, who seemed to have taken early retirement, liked to observe my activities as I cut the bodies and sanded them, warming the wood, or threaded the holes in the wings and body with plastic fishing line. Which was exactly what I was doing on a late fall evening in 1982 when the basement began to flood. I'd just turned thirteen.

It had rained the night before and all morning, afternoon, all through dinner too. A record rain, we'd later find out. Our basement began to flood, not some shallow dampness but a floating, threatening flood that eventually reached up to our ankles.

"Turn the pump off!" my mother yelled, but it made no difference, the water kept rising, bubbling up over the lip of the well, seeping in from the walls until our river had become a lake.

The insurance company refused to pay for the clean up. It wasn't their fault, they said, that someone had diverted an underground creek through their household basement, an assessment my mother was all to ready to agree with, at least to Duncan.

"What were you thinking!" Emily bawled, forgetting that she'd once posed with my father for the picture in the newspaper: *Duncan and Emily Gray, standing beside their river*.

Duncan, out of impotent embarrassment and a stern command from my mother, absented himself from the negotiations with the insurance company but overheard, as I did, her skilful manoeuvring; she had a way of denouncing my father to the insurance agents without making him liable. A local government official, called in by the insurance company, made an inspection and threatened to bring charges against my father for tampering with municipal sewage drains. The city finally let the matter drop so long as Duncan promised never to divert water into his basement again.

Workmen came to do the repairs. They filled in the well, trampled through the riverbed, and tossed the heavy stones my father and I had carried out of the forest into a Dumpster full of rotting drywall, wood, and rusted nails. They liberally sprinkled a powder-white disinfectant that smelled sweetly poisonous, and graded the basement floor with new concrete so that, when they were finished, there was no evidence left of my father's creation.

Because of the flood, my mother was exposed to the insurance company's assessment of our house. Her astonishment at its value helped temper the full rage she felt toward Duncan and drove her to get a real-estate licence.

"Somebody has to make the money around here," she said. And she began to do so immediately by helping the Hungarians and Portuguese in our neighbourhood sell their homes at fat profits and move away.

Duncan had nowhere to hide any more. When he came downstairs to watch me make birds he'd stand in the dry, clean basement like a man who'd just stepped off a ship and was trying to find his legs.

Teetering on the concrete, Duncan asked for a cigarette. I'd begun to smoke, a habit my mother deplored and my father tolerated, but which neither of them, being smokers themselves, was in the position to forbid. I liked the feel of the tinfoil – the tug and pull of it and the rigid, uniform rows of tobacco trees, like a planted forest all lined up for harvesting.

"I've never meant to do the things that I've done," he suddenly said to me, opening a window before striking his match. "It was the river."

"It's gone now," I said. But was it? Maybe it was just hidden. If I closed my eyes and stopped breathing I was certain I could hear its watery march toward the lake.

"At least your birds are safe." My father stared up at the ceiling, where my birds floated above our heads, in clouds of tobacco smoke. "Nothing else survived the flood."

"They're seagulls," I said. They were born for the water.

# Unanticipated Risks

FROM THE CABINET over the bathroom sink I pulled out my bottle of folic acid. Dr. Henderson had written me a prescription on a medical notepad that I'd handed over to the pharmacist with the minor embarrassment I always felt whenever I was at the mercy of somebody else's expertise. When I was told I could find what I was looking for in the regular vitamin section of the store, I had gone to look for my pills with a growing sense of skepticism, questioning the medicinal strength of anything that sat on the same shelf as Flintstones multivitamins.

It was Julia who was taking the real drugs. She'd started going to the clinic every day to be injected with Puregon to increase the size and number of her follicles so that, when the time came, she'd be more receptive to my fragile sperm.

The bathroom door was unlocked, but Julia stood on the other side and waited impatiently for my exit. "Hurry up, I'm late."

There was only one bathroom in the house, a fact neither of us had minded when we'd moved in – there'd only been one bathroom in Julia's apartment – but, on occasion, it could cause irritation.

"In a minute," I called out, washing a pill down with a cupped hand of water.

I screwed the cap back on and returned the bottle to the lower right corner of the cabinet – my small space of bathroom real estate – and felt diminished over what I considered the ineffectiveness of my pills and the cramped space they sat in, emblematic, I thought, of the way I felt about our house.

Shortly after our marriage my mother had suggested Julia and I stop renting and buy. "I'll find the perfect spot," she'd said. Naturally there wouldn't be any commission. This appealed to Julia; why pay rent when we could apply that money to a mortgage? Reluctant to have my mother involved in any part of my life, I sat sulkily in the back of her VW Jetta that smelled of leather and polish and spotless success, its illuminated dashboard orange like a Day-Glo sunrise, as she escorted us to sturdily pitched FOR SALE signs in desirable yet affordable neighbourhoods.

Emily was relentless. She sold real estate with the same dogmatic conviction with which she'd previously pursued human rights, as if each house was an ideology worthy of acceptance. The same woman who'd allowed a river to be built in her basement now managed to convey to her clients – the latest ones being her son and daughter-in-law – that houses were permanent and stable and could only bring great happiness.

For every one of my objections, my mother offered a fitting answer.

"What if we bought a house and then decided we'd made a mistake?"

"You can sell at a profit."

"What if interest rates went up?"

"Lock in."

Utilities, insurance?

There are special plans, not to worry, everything is manageable. Houses, according to my mother, weren't there to betray you, but to protect you.

*Just like a mother is supposed to*, I thought grimly.

I didn't have the money to make a down payment on a house. Everything I had was tied up in the bird factory, which had recently moved from its cramped downtown location to the suburbs. If, as I liked to imagine, the birds had led me to Julia, then Julia had led me to the storks and a doubling of my business. I actually employed people. But I didn't have any money, not for a house anyway.

"I do," Julia had said.

So here I was in a house, which was mine and yet not mine, swallowing little pills, which might or might not help, trying to get my wife pregnant, which might or might not happen.

"Hurry up!" Julia shouted. She had another appointment at the clinic this morning and that gave her undisputed priority.

"I'm coming, I'm coming."

"If I don't get there on time they make you wait forever as punishment," she said through the door. "You can't believe how rude the nurses are. You'd think they'd be more understanding, but I get the sense they hate us."

The urgency in her voice was cover for the anxiety I knew she felt about the clinic. Julia overcame unpleasantness with *busyness*. When she felt overwhelmed, her antidote was to overwhelm herself even more, in contrast to my own method, which was often to drop everything and take to my bed in depression.

These were our little differences, I reflected, opening the door to let her in. She rushed past me, saying, "I have an important meeting after the clinic. A CEO was caught with two underage girls in Costa Rica and the company is about to launch an IPO in less than a month. Having a CEO in a Costa Rican jail isn't the best way to raise share price."

"No, I suppose it isn't."

Ready, I walked downstairs, extricated my car and house keys that lay entwined with Julia's in the ceramic bowl by the front door, and called out a goodbye, conscious that the twinge of inadequacy I'd felt earlier had returned.

It was clear which job was the more lucrative; I made wooden birds, Julia developed sophisticated speaking points for pedophilic corporate executives. She was good at her job, but despite her encouragement to expand my business, Julia still hadn't left the company she disliked to start one of her own. Her objections, that it would take a lot of money and it might not work, were reasonable enough except that barring some global economic calamity, I couldn't imagine Julia failing; she was too dedicated, too organized, too strong.

"You can't just do what you want when you want it. No matter how good your business plan, there are always unanticipated risks, risks we can't afford to take right now."

*Because the bird factory doesn't bring in enough money.* That's what Julia had meant. I thought about this as I drove the grey, congested highways out to Mississauga and the bird factory. Pulling into the parking lot at the factory, I spotted Mr. Chang, my industrial neighbour, waiting outside for another shipments of lamps, clipboard in hand, just as he'd done for fifteen years. Their warehouse had lamps of every size and style: wall lamps, floor lamps, lamps with fans on them, lamps shaped like flower petals, lamps for the bathroom, the kitchen, the dining room. Each lamp was wrapped in a protective sheet of plastic, a sort of lamp condom. Lamps.

Mrs. Chang came out to join her husband, who was always anxious when new deliveries arrived, and I waved at her through the car window. I'd made them a flying dragon to celebrate the longevity of their business and, as I parked my car, I wondered how I would feel if I spent fifteen years here making birds and then had the Changs come over with a gift lamp. *Unanticipated risk*, I thought.

Philip was already at the bird factory, working on one of the jumbos. He liked putting in the extra effort and concentration because each jumbo bird was unique, a one-off. If Philip had been another sort of person, he'd probably have said he liked the artistic freedom of designing his own birds, but he wasn't that sort of person so he didn't say much of anything.

"Everything all right?" I asked, throwing my keys down on the worktable.

"Yup."

Philip. He'd walked into the bird factory one day, about six months after I'd moved to suburban Mississauga, asking if I needed any help. Just driving around, he said, seeing if anyone needed him.

A little over thirty but looking well into his forties, Philip had deeply recessed eyes – two glossy black balls set in snooker-like pockets. A mangy beard made his face look vandalized, and he walked like an old man, with hands swivelled out as if he was paddling the air. I hired him because he'd struck me as no better or worse than anyone else I'd hired before. But Philip turned out to be different from all the others.

He cared about the birds.

Within the first month of working for me, he'd devised a series of ropes and pulleys to hoist a line of weighted birds up to the ceiling, freeing up space below, and began taking jumbo birds home with him so he could work on them during the evenings. At lunch breaks, he'd talk about work – how many bird wings he'd dunked in paint, the number of precut bird bodies we'd need for the week, a shop he'd passed that looked as if they might want a bird or two.

Before Philip, whomever I hired had never lasted beyond two months. They'd slouch in with pierced septum and inked skin, learn the bare necessities, and then, at their convenience, casually announce they'd found a better job. I'd moved out to Mississauga for the cheap industrial rents and the thought – hard to believe now – that the suburbs would provide me with an unending supply of stable employees.

My inevitable irritation at their departure was always deepened by a sense, no matter how unfounded, of abandonment. I'd tell myself that their resignation had nothing to do with me, but with the work itself, that the bird factory was just an unremarkable, if unexpected, passage in their lives, but deep down I felt they were just passing through the factory, through me, past me, while I remained forever behind, perpetually condemned to making birds that flew off like the hired help.

I should have been grateful for Philip. I *was* grateful. I also saw him as a contemptible idiot who made birds for a living. The fact that Philip appeared uninterested in moving on, that he was a loyal, dedicated employee who never complained if he had to work late, who actually made suggestions and added value to the company, only heightened my contempt for him. He was like Boxer from *Animal Farm* – a workhorse forever abused.

"Where's Hans?" I asked.

"He's not here."

"Obviously. Did he phone?"

Philip snorted.

"I'll say something about it when he gets in," I said.

Hans worked at the bird factory twice a week. He was never on time and I always talked to him about it and it never made any difference. Hans called me the Little Dictator. He referred to Philip as Lurch. Somehow the names had stuck.

"If he doesn't come soon we'll run out of bird parts." Philip pulled down on the rope and hoisted one of the jumbo storks he'd been working on up to the ceiling. They always looked better up there; they were meant to be seen from below.

"I'll talk to him," I repeated and walked to my office, which was a desk, a phone, and a metal filing cabinet pushed up against the wall and located less than five feet away from where Philip was working.

The bird factory inhabited 1,250 square feet of industrial space divided into four areas. There was the cut room, which contained two blade saws, one band saw, and wads of sandpaper and, beside it, the paint room, where the bodies and wings were dipped in paint, then pinned to clotheslines and dried. These were the rooms where Hans usually worked. When he was finished cutting, sanding, and painting, he passed the birds down the hallway, toward the front of the building, where Philip tied them up in the bird assembly room before escorting them into the weight room, which we were in now, to balance their wings and package them up.

At least it looked organized. In truth, the bird factory was, like the suburb of Mississauga in which it was situated, distinctly zoned yet chaotic, ill planned, and confusing. There were always problems – shortages of parts, broken equipment, and late employees.

Bird making – of this I was certain – was a curse I'd picked up from using my father's tools. I'd always found it somewhat astonishing that by combining my father's tools and my own unhappiness I could make something beautiful and wanted. My mother had started to offer them as housewarming gifts to her real-estate clients, their friends called and placed orders, and in time I began to see that I couldn't shake the birds loose. It was as if they'd imprinted on me. I kept making them, people kept buying them. I was always promising myself that I would stop, but I never did.

Julia insisted the bird factory wasn't a curse, it was a business, a viable, expandable, successful mobile bird-making business. Any problems I might have, she said, stemmed from having made birds as a child. Over the years I'd grown the company in an ad hoc fashion. She pointed out that most of my sales still came from word of mouth and that I hired people I neither liked nor fully expected to last the year. She said I needed to keep track of inventory, make long-range projections, buy in bigger bulk, drive harder bargains with my suppliers, and bring down costs. She thought all her suggestions were obtainable and obvious and something I would have done long ago if I hadn't started making birds before my adolescence and didn't believe – childishly, she insisted – that the birds were a curse.

Hans walked through the front door.

"You're late, Hans."

"Can you blame me?"

"Yes, I can."

"Who would ever want to be here on time, except for Lurch, who never wants to leave."

Philip ignored him.

"Put on your coveralls, and get to work," I said. "We have orders to fill."

I picked up the phone and called a supplier, hoping that Hans would get the hint; instead, he pulled a cigarette from his breast pocket, lit it, and ignited within me a horrendous craving to have one myself. I'd promised Julia I would quit smoking. I hadn't succeeded. But I was trying, and trying meant never having a cigarette with Hans because, though he couldn't possibly know about my promise to quit, I didn't want to show any weakness in front of him.

Born in Leipzig, Hans had moved to Berlin, then London, because his boyfriend was British and he'd wanted to learn English, then to Toronto, to follow another boyfriend, and finally to Mississauga, where he'd followed, so far as I knew, no one but himself. When he got the job, Hans rented a small studio in the same complex that housed the bird factory. He lived there, though it went against the conditions of the lease, sleeping on a small cot he hid beneath the enormous canvases he used for his paintings. The one time I'd been to his studio, I'd noticed that all his paintings were the same: long, wide, perfectly smooth ribbons of empty suburban road reaching out toward the distant horizon.

Hans was gay. Old school. Gay relationships bored him, which perhaps explained why he'd ended up alone in the suburbs of Toronto, and State-sanctioned gay marriage repelled him. Why would gay men want to be like everyone else? He thought people like me were pitiful, courting the same body night after night, fearful of being alone, fearful of contracting a disease, fearful of being themselves. Being gay was the truest expression of being a man – that's what Hans thought. He got "spiked" each and every weekend. At will. At random. With whomever he pleased and sometimes not even that.

And he showed up twice a week at the factory and made wooden birds. He couldn't forgive me for that but, almost despite himself, he'd given my birds a lustre and sheen they'd never before had.

After getting off the phone with my supplier, I called several stores that carried our birds, to see if they wanted to place any new orders. Philip and Hans made most of the birds now; I went around trying to sell them. I sold the birds to maternity stores, department stores, convenience stores, furniture stores, arts and craft stores, children's stores, even a few art galleries, which was how I'd been introduced to Hans. A gallery owner had informed me about a painter who had recently emigrated from Germany via London, searching for part-time work.

Hans was still behind me, but in the interval of time he'd put on his work clothes, a dirty red flightsuit that made him look like a failed Luftwaffe mechanic. He'd finished his cigarette and was just standing there.

"I would like to speak to you about a raise."

"Now?"

"Yes, of course. I am asking you now."

"But you just came in late. You think this is the best time to ask for a raise?"

"If you paid your employees more money, they would come in more on time."

"Hans, there is just you, me, and Philip, and two of us manage to get here on time."

"You are often not on time."

"Sometimes –" I stopped myself. "This is my company, Hans. And I can do what I like. I don't have to explain myself to you. Now, please, fuck off and get to work."

"We're almost out of painted wings," Philip added, distressed. In the past, I'd mockingly called Philip my production manager, but quickly dropped the title after he'd requested business cards. He couldn't understand why I didn't fire Hans. He would have happily done it himself if I'd let him.

Eventually, Hans began his retreat toward the painting room.

"This is not a good place," he said.

I looked over at Philip, who pulled a red-and-blue ribbon dangling down from the belly of a seagull, setting in motion a gentle flapping of its wings. It seemed to soothe him.

These were my two employees, the first two who'd stuck around for more than a few months – Philip because he seemed peculiarly dedicated and Hans because he hated me and stayed, I was convinced, only to torture me.

I spent the morning on the phone, then packaged up the birds in small boxes and bubble envelopes, writing down the addresses of places I'd never been: San Jose, California; Manchester, England; Chicago, Illinois. My birds flew great distances.

"I'm off to the post office," I told Philip when I was finished. "Then I'm going to deliver some birds."

Philip nodded.

"Need anything?"

"No."

"You sure?"

"Yeah."

After mailing my packages, I drove back into the city and started my delivery rounds, mostly to small stores that sold one or two birds every six months or so. I had no intention of returning to the factory that afternoon. Instead, after handing over the last of my storks to a high-end maternity store that marked up my birds a full twenty per cent above anywhere else in the city, I returned home, wondering if Julia had arrived at the clinic on time and if the nurses had been pleasant or rude. When we'd first started trying for a baby, long before I found her upside down in the bed, long before Dr. Henderson had introduced himself and informed me I had lazy sperm, she'd said her company offered maternity leave and security. It was the sort of security she needed, now that we'd just bought a house and had a mortgage to pay.

*Now that we were trying to have a baby.*

Unlocking the front door to the house I did not own and that my mother had found, I admitted to myself that I'd always been wary of moving from Julia's apartment, where we'd been so happy, into this place that – fine as it was with solid, double-brick walls and a deep, dry, stone-encased basement that had, throughout all its ninety-odd years, successfully repulsed the damp, black earth – felt like a risk. And I admitted to myself too that I was wary of having a baby. Who knew what could be waiting for us around the next corner?

Julia's startled voice called out from the living room.

"Luke?"

Julia hardly ever arrived home before me. "What are you doing here?" I asked.

"I could ask the same of you."

"I decided to knock off early."

"Me too."

"Are you all right?" I asked, taking off my shoes, but she didn't answer. "Julia?"

# Other People's Problems

I FOUND JULIA AND MY MOTHER seated together on the living-room couch. Found is perhaps the wrong word, since all I'd had to do was open my front door, walk a few feet forward, turn left and stare at them, but it wasn't unlike finding two mismatched socks hidden together beneath the bed. Each one belonged to me, just not together.

My mother, in contrast to Julia, beamed with intrusive pleasure. There was something protective and deceitful about her smile, as if she was attempting to compensate for Julia's startled expression.

"What are you doing here?" I demanded.

"Does your mother need a reason to be at her son and daughter-in-law's house?"

*Actually, yes.*

"Julia and I are just having a chat," my mother said, noticing my expression.

"Then I won't intrude."

I walked quietly into the kitchen and poured myself a glass of filtered water.

"You don't have any messages," Julia called out. She knew my habits. Each day after work I poured myself a drink, listened to my messages, and then, if I hadn't already done so that morning, sat down on the couch and read the newspaper that Julia had refolded and placed on the small coffee table. I used to smoke a cigarette, which I now tended to do on the drive home rather than in my living room.

These were part of the small constancies of marriage that I felt brought a certain order, even decency, to my life. My mother was not part of my routine; I didn't like finding her on my living-room couch. And I didn't like her sneaking up behind me.

"I hear you're lazy," she said.

I offered a correction. "No, Mom, my sperm are lazy."

I went over to the fridge and opened it. The brightly lit, stocked world of food momentarily lifted my anxiety.

"What kind of diagnosis is lazy sperm? It sounds like one of those English bands you listened to as a teenager."

"Where's Julia?"

"Upstairs peeing," my mother answered authoritatively, as if my wife had done so on her insistence.

"This isn't your business,' I said, holding on to the fridge door – it was either that or strangle her.

"You know," my mother continued, "it's the funniest thing. In my day, we were all fearful of getting pregnant. You can't imagine what the pill meant for us. The freedom. Now, everyone's waiting for a pill to *make* them pregnant." My mother mentioned the names of several of her friends, all of whom had offspring unable to conceive. "It seems people your age can't have babies."

Hearing Julia's descent, my mother spun around and marched herself back into the living room. I followed behind with short, hostile steps. She stopped, turned, and whispered, "Don't blame her. She needed someone to talk to. A woman."

She moved forward again, a relentless surge, her hands reaching out for Julia's.

"Luke understands exactly why you needed to talk to me," she said, guiding Julia to the couch and sitting her down. "And I've been thinking about what you told me and I don't believe the doctor's diagnosis is entirely correct. Luke's sperm aren't lazy, they're reclusive. He was like that right from the beginning, always shielding himself from anything that was out of the ordinary. I remember trying to get him to eat Indian food." My mother rolled her eyes at the thought. "He always shunned the new, feared the unknown. It was almost instinctual, as if his life depended on keeping order. His father called him 'our little Prussian.'"

My mother suddenly consulted her watch. "I have to show a house," she said and took Julia's hand again, to let herself be escorted to the front door. "But I have a good feeling about all this. You were right to talk to me, you can't keep something like this inside of you. It will be fine, we just need to get Luke's sperm out of their shell, give them a sense of adventure."

I pushed my mother out the door.

When we returned to the living room I confronted my wife. "Telling my mother I'm infertile is probably not good for our marriage."

"It wasn't my fault, Luke, I came home early because I was feeling a bit tired from all the drugs, and your mother showed up. We were sitting down having tea" – Julia pointed toward the tray of cups and saucers on the side table as if in evidence of her good faith – "and when the phone rang I let the answering machine pick up and it was the clinic. Your mother heard the message and started asking questions. And you're not infertile. You just have a low sperm count."

I was suspicious. Julia hardly ever returned early from work and she never let the answering machine pick up when she was home. We'd had arguments about this. Let it ring, I'd say, if it's important they'll leave a message. But for Julia a ringing phone was the equivalent of a police officer pounding on the front door, an imperative command that needed to be answered.

"You didn't tell her everything, did you?"

"Your mother can be so persuasive. She made me feel that I needed to talk to someone. And she was right, I did."

Julia walked over to the fireplace, pulled out a match from a box above the mantle, crouched down and set alight the prepared kindling. Julia loved fires, lit them in all but the hottest months.

"You can talk to me if you need to talk to someone."

"But you don't want to talk." Julia stared at the fire. "It's hard going to the fertility clinic by myself."

"I've offered to go with you, but you told me there was no reason to sit in the waiting room with nothing to do. You said it would be just like waiting for the kettle to boil."

And that made perfect sense to me. I might even be a hindrance, slowing her down with my own worries and irritations.

"I didn't want you to come because I can tell you really don't want to."

"Of course I don't want to! Who would want to go to a fertility clinic?"

Peeling away from the chimney, like a crack of lightning, was a narrow, detectable fissure that ran along the ceiling. I'd patched up the fissure the year before, but now it was back and growing. How many times had I told Julia to ease up on the fires? Heat from the chimney radiated into the plaster causing it to expand and then, as it cooled, to retract, pulling apart the imperceptible molecular handshakes that kept the surface firm and smooth.

I watched the flames from Julia's fire spark and grow, stoking the rebellion above our heads. She made the heat that made the crack that pointed, however obliquely, to the disorder I felt was engulfing me.

"I'd go to the clinic with you if you asked, but you haven't asked, so I haven't gone."

"Exactly."

I walked to the window and stared out toward the vacant space on the street left behind by my mother's car, noting with some bitterness that Julia had no intention of taking our problems to her own family that was too good, too proper, too respectable for unpleasant news. She would disturb neither her mother nor her father with our fertility problems, and she certainly couldn't talk to her younger brother, Barry. There was a part of me that wondered if it was partly *because* of Barry that Julia didn't want to go to her parents. Barry had been born with

Down syndrome and at twenty-six had only just moved out of his parents' home and into a special residential community where he could gain a small measure of independence.

The Riddells didn't talk much about Barry, whom they loved but kept their distance from as they kept their distance from everybody else, including each other. I found him repugnant and poignant, in the sort of way people who aren't comfortable with the handicapped often do. At first I'd referred to Barry's condition with an arsenal of euphemisms like *mentally disabled*, *developmentally challenged*, *learning disabled*, but his father insisted otherwise. "The boy's retarded!" According to Lloyd Riddell, it's what Barry was called twenty-six years ago when he was born, what he was today, would be tomorrow, and continue to be until the day he died.

Barry might have been retarded, but he wasn't stupid. From the beginning he'd been suspicious of me. He'd picked up my tone of false interest: "That's a nice shirt you're wearing, Barry," "So, Barry, how do you like your new school?" "Seen any good movies?" He knew I didn't care, that I even found him repulsive because there was, in his fleshy, disorganized face, a hint of Julia, the woman I loved, staring back at me.

Disturbed by the image, I walked to the kitchen and poured myself another drink of filtered water, morbidly pleased at the maturity I exhibited by not reaching for something stronger, and recalled the first time I'd met Barry. He'd said I wasn't like his sister's last boyfriend; it wasn't a compliment. Barry's parents also thought I wasn't like her last boyfriend; that wasn't a compliment either. "Oh, you make mobile birds," Maureen Riddell had remarked with the same note of false interest I reserved for her retarded son.

Julia's parents lived in North Toronto, an area encompassing a wide number of neighbourhoods that shared, apart from a general geographical location, a number of similar attributes. The houses had been built primarily between the wars, with porticos but no verandas because any leisure activity was to remain strictly out of sight. All had large backyards, fenceless yet crisply bordered front yards too, composed mostly of grass and maybe a few flowerbeds and hedges lining the pathway to their sheltered front doors.

As a child I used to look out of the back car window with longing at the owners tending their properties – the women wearing gardening gloves, the men in baseball caps – and imagine that they would see me peering out the window and recognize my face. Duncan might be at a Stop sign and they'd walk over, lean into the open car window, and calmly request that Duncan and Emily give me back, which they would do because – all of us laughing now – we'd recognize there'd been some sort of mistake. But sometimes I imagined that Duncan wasn't idling at a Stop sign but speeding down the street, setting off two-toned alarms that sounded like the French police, alerting the good, sensible citizens of North Toronto to the intrusion. Furious crowds would chase us down, pull Duncan and Emily out of the car, and beat them mercilessly.

I think a lot of unhappy children have dreams like that.

At the Riddells, there was a startling – and, I must add, deeply admirable – lack of conversational vitality. Anything of consequence or importance was simply not discussed except in the driest let's-solve-the-problem sort of way; and since, in their opinion, most of the important and consequential things in this world had no solution, they thought it best not to say very much about anything.

Which was not to suggest silence; they talked about house prices and interest rates, what they'd eaten for supper that evening, and the upcoming needs Julia and I might have for new furnishings, which was of particular interest to Mrs. Riddell because she was an interior decorator with, from what I could discern, a client base of exactly one – herself – but the Riddells employed words in ways I'd rarely encountered before. Words were not used to convey or inflict suffering, to offer personal complaints, or to astonish.

They were my ideal family.

I remembered my acute discomfort the first and only time our two families had collided in the Riddells' living room, shortly after my marriage to Julia. Duncan, trying to impress Lloyd, went on about his teaching job at Ryerson as if nothing gave him more enjoyment and satisfaction, while Maureen spoke of garden furniture to a glazed-eyed Emily. Under normal circumstances, neither my mother nor my father would have dreamed of stepping into a place like this – too monied, too bourgeois, too boring, too dull. *They're in enemy territory*, I thought. They should be rising up in protest. But they stayed on until they could politely make their getaway, leaving me behind, a full-fledged, card-carrying member of the Riddell clan.

Julia turned and faced me from her spot by the fireplace, holding her hands behind her back, warming them, though the house was far from cold.

"I'm going to be ready soon. For insemination. That's why the clinic phoned when your mother was here."

"That's good."

"I guess I'm scared."

"Me too," I nodded.

I was always scared. I was scared of so many things I hadn't had time to be scared for Julia. She was alone and I suddenly felt terribly sorry for her.

The Riddells still thought of me as a bird-maker, unworthy of their daughter's choice for a husband, and who could blame them. What they didn't know was that I was a bird-maker with lazy sperm who couldn't get their daughter pregnant without outside assistance; that their only daughter rose each morning, showered with soap that smelled of green apples, dressed with nervous attention, and drove off to be treated with fertility drugs that made her eggs grow and multiply to artificial proportions so that, as Dr. Henderson had indelicately put it, all my bad marksmen would have bigger targets to fire at.

To me, Julia's body had always been as easily defined, as bordered and trim, as the Riddells' front lawn, but I wondered if, when Julia traced the outline of her body with her apple-scented soap, the immutability of those borders was a source of sadness. For her, unchanging stability now meant failure.

No wonder Julia gravitated toward my family. The Riddells were people of boundaries. You needed a passport before you crossed over. Baggage needed to be inspected, duties paid. But there weren't any boundaries at the Gray residence, no border inspections or visa requirements, just a wide open plain where the world's problems could pass through unmolested.

# I Needed Things

"IT'S TIME."

Julia pushed open the bedroom door with her foot and carried a large breakfast tray into the room. A funnel of steam rose from the coffee cup.

"Your favourites," Julia said, pinning me to the bed with the tray. There were three eggs, sunnyside up, six strips of bacon, two slices of toast, cut diagonally and spread with butter and jam, a pot of coffee, and one still-rolled-up newspaper. "I hope you enjoy it."

In the right corner of the wooden tray, with its painted trellis of budding roses – a birthday present given to me by my mother-in-law – sat a small plastic vial with a blue top. Instead of the vacuum-packed, super-sterilized test tube of my imagination, there was before me a simple plastic container that looked no more sterile than a kitchen glass.

Julia had printed my name in her forbiddingly neat handwriting on the affixed label: *Luke Gray*. Below, machine-stamped, the words SAMPLE TIME ______. The darkly inked, imposing line waiting to be filled in.

Julia's eggs were ready for fertilization. They'd been *stimulated*, to use the clinic's description, with Puregon, to assist my sperm, which after a rich breakfast full of enhancing carbohydrates, I could provide from the comforts of my own home, as long as it was delivered to the clinic within half an hour.

Julia watched with calculating eyes as I mopped up the last of my eggs with the toast. All this food was delivered to me in bed by my wife, yet it had nothing to do with me. I'd become, somehow, subservient to myself.

"So," she said, sidling up beside me. "Are you going to fly solo today?"

For a moment we just stared at each other. I told her I wasn't sure, I hadn't thought it through.

"It's your call," she said and then, probably aware of the slight impatience in her voice, said, "I have a big meeting afterwards. It was booked last week. I couldn't cancel it."

I looked down at the vial. It was very small, no taller than my thumb, and only marginally wider than an erect penis. *So easy to make a mistake*, I thought. And then where would we be? Julia was wearing a business suit, a not wholly appropriate outfit for a couple about to attempt an intimate act.

I told Julia it was better to put business before pleasure.

"I'll leave you alone." She reached for the tray and I suddenly felt abandoned.

"Remember those little mermaids you could send away for?" I said. "All the sea monkeys had little crowns on their heads and wands in their hands. Remember?"

"I think they were tridents." Julia looked at her watch.

"I begged my father to get them. My mother was in the middle of one of her disappearances and all I thought about, every day, almost every moment, were sea monkeys. Duncan eventually ordered the entire set, with the extra swings and waterslides and I filled up the plastic aquarium with water from the basement river, poured in this freeze-dried stuff, and waited and waited and waited until I grew hysterical because nothing was happening. My poor father was so upset he phoned the company to yell at them."

Julia shifted the weight of the tray. "I'm going now. Make me sea monkeys."

"Okay."

"I don't have all that much time, so hurry up."

I answered with honesty that I'd do my best and watched Julia aerobically hook the door with her left foot and sharply close it behind her. She'd left two things behind: the newspaper, filled with the disposable news of the day, and the plastic vial, which she'd conscientiously placed on my night table while I'd been eating. I picked up the newspaper.

It wasn't all that surprising. Now that I was involved in fertility treatments I found references to them everywhere. On the bottom fold of page A18 was the story of Dr. Henry Kilpatrick, of Orange County, California, who'd been indicted for replacing his patients' sperm with his own. According to the article, this explained why the success rates at his world-renowned fertility clinic exceeded national norms. Authorities were actively seeking all of Dr. Kilpatrick's former patients, but many already contacted had refused DNA tests to determine paternity. "God gave us our child," said one couple, "not Dr. Kilpatrick," which, religious sentiment aside, struck me as beside the point. I remembered reading somewhere that babies look like their father for the first six months, to mitigate the murderous, doubting impulses that lurked in the breast of every male. There wasn't a picture of the doctor in the newspaper, but they knew what he looked like and perhaps in time would see the truth staring at them with loving eyes.

The phone rang. It was my mother, voice strident with bad news, alerting me to the article.

"I've just read something terrible," she said. "There's a fertility doctor who's using his own sperm to impregnate his patients!"

I gazed out the bedroom window and thought of Julia, whom I'd watched pedal away to the fertility clinic only moments before. It was a hot summer's day and Julia had decided to take her bicycle, tucking business shoes and sperm vial into her satchel. There was something odd about watching Julia push off to the clinic on a bicycle, like watching an astronaut pedal toward her space ship.

It was possible the vial wasn't in her satchel. It might be tucked under her breast or inside her front pocket, to keep it warm, as the clinic had recommended. I suddenly panicked, wondering if it would be *too* warm pressed up against her sweating, overheated body. Surely, on such a hot day, the idea was to keep it cool. I really didn't know where she put it, and there was something odd about that too. After reading about Dr. Kilpatrick I'd put the paper down and got on with the business at hand, so to speak, and then, as directed, I'd screwed on the blue cap and written down the time of my deposit.

There it was, a watery, goopy, insubstantial mass of defective sperm. I was aware of the imbalance between pleasure and its result, but the see-through vial quantified the outcome in ways I found unsettling – there was so little when there should have been so much. That was all of me in there, all I had to give. And it barely filled the bottom of the vial. Men get out of the habit of examining their sperm shortly after their first ejaculation and it's a shame they do because it's a humbling experience. This was what it was all about, passing oneself down the line. What else was there? Making more birds? Or toothpaste or television shows?

I hadn't told Julia, when she'd come upstairs to collect the goods, about the newspaper article, but I don't think it would have bothered her. There was something far too workmanlike about Julia to let some doctor in Orange County distract her. She'd entered the bedroom, pen in hand, ready to write down the time of deposit, and seemed almost put out that I'd already done so, as if I'd overstepped the bounds of my authority.

"It's all done," I said.

Julia kissed me with distracted lips and took the vial from my hands without looking at it. I wondered is she was embarrassed. Maybe, on her way, she'd take a look. I bet she'd be surprised by its insubstantiveness. Disappointed, perhaps?

It didn't feel right that my potential offspring should be held captive in a cheap plastic vial. Something more appropriate, a silver chalice or crystal glass – anything with some value or worth – would have been better.

I shouldn't have refused Julia's assistance in the bedroom, but in my one primary act of creation I'd wanted to be left untouched by outside assistance or influence. Perhaps other couples in similar circumstances were better able to make a game of it, or use the experience of fertility treatments to become more united. I couldn't be sure if Julia was hurt or relieved that I'd wanted to be alone. Maybe it was both.

Julia hadn't wanted me to accompany her to the fertility clinic either. I tried to insist, given what she'd said about my lack of participation, but I guess she could tell my heart wasn't in it, because she refused my offer, saying there'd be little for me to do but sit around and read outdated magazines while she, a nurse, and Dr. Henderson busied themselves behind closed doors.

For the past several weeks, Julia had been going to the clinic early in the morning, before work, where her follicles were inspected by ultrasound and drugs were administered to promote their growth. The drugs also affected Julia's mood. She said it was like having her hormones connected to an espresso machine.

In our fridge was a packet of progesterone, a hormone the fertility clinic had prescribed for her. It sat on the upper shelf, beside the filtered water, its long cardboard box looking like a container for toothpaste but without the flashy colours; just plain white with the drug's name printed in light blue on two sides. They were suppositories that Julia told me were used to help her fertilized eggs stick to her uterus.

"Like Velcro?"

Julia, who'd taken to wearing her hair in pigtails after work and looked like a twelve-year-old who hadn't been sleeping very well, explained, "When a woman's eggs travel down the Fallopian tubes, they drop into the uterus and often, thanks to gravity, just keep on going. Progesterone somehow makes them stick."

I often felt that way about Julia, that if I became detached from her I would be swept down and away, by forces outside of my control.

*I should have gone with her*, I thought. *It would have been the right thing to do.*

"And do you know why he did it?" my mother continued, undeterred by my silence, "Dr. Kilpatrick said the need to advertise high live birth rates, whatever that means, compelled him to replace the husbands' defective sperm with his own. He was compelled! And do you know why? And here I quote: 'Acknowledging the pain and suffering his actions might have caused, Dr. Kilpatrick said that his competitive instincts usurped his professional judgment.'" My mother paused. Then she said, "That's men for you."

I determined that clothes – at least some underwear – were in order and snatched up yesterday's boxers from the floor beside my bed.

"They can't help themselves. Men have to stick their thing into everything, even when all they're sticking it into is a test tube. But I don't want you to worry," she said. "Dr. Henderson is a good doctor."

"I'm not worried," I answered. And I wasn't. I'd found the article soothing, like reading about a plane crash shortly before boarding a flight; the narrow maw of statistical probability had bitten down and claimed its month's allotment of victims.

And then something my mother had said caught my attention.

"How do you know that Dr. Henderson is a good doctor?" I asked.

"Oh, well, I just do . . ." My mother's voice, only seconds ago vociferous and clear, trailed off into a whisper.

"How?"

She hesitated.

"I sold him a house."

"You sold my fertility specialist a house?" It seemed like a remarkable coincidence.

"Don't tell Julia," my mother pleaded.

"Don't tell her what?"

"Don't tell her I told you. I shouldn't have said anything. It's my fault."

"Julia knows?"

"I offered to help. I called him up. The man has an eight-month waiting list! How else do you think you got to see him? And I know he's a good doctor because you can tell a lot about someone when they're buying a house. Some people tell you what they're looking for but never like what you show them even when it matches their description perfectly. And some people don't tell you anything and get annoyed at everything you show them. Others never put in the right bid and are constantly disappointed and surprised when they don't get the house. But Dr. Henderson told me what he wanted, looked at several high-end properties in Rosedale, found the one he was looking for, made the right offer, and thanked me for my services. It's a lovely four-bedroom with a kidney-shaped pool and excellently landscaped. I know you can trust a man like him."

"I just can't trust you," I said, thinking, as I hung up the phone, that I couldn't trust my wife either. Julia's entire explanation for how my mother had found out about our fertility problems was a lie. Emily hadn't overheard a voice message from the clinic that day I'd found her and Julia in the living room. My mother had been in on it from the beginning.

This was how Julia went about her business. You spoke to people, you used your contacts, found out what they knew and how they could help you. If you don't know where you're going, ask for directions. That was Julia's viewpoint. Only, I didn't like it when other people knew where I was going; I certainly didn't want them to know I was lost. Julia might have believed that what she had done was perfectly rational, and successful – my mother had, through her own network, found us a good doctor with a kidney-shaped swimming pool – but there was nothing rational about standing in my underwear, angry and depleted, worrying if my sperm vial was overheating and listening to my mother recount the newspaper story of a rogue fertility specialist.

I twisted the blinds closed, took off my underwear, crawled back into bed. And worried. What if the vial *was* overheating? *We're already talking about weak sperm*, I thought. *Genetically deficient.* Maybe they'd make a Barry. Could I handle it? Julia had what seemed to me an almost unlimited capacity for love, witness her affection for her brother. But it went beyond that. Just recently, she'd signed up as a reader at the Hospital for

Sick Children. Julia worked twice as hard as me, but she rushed over and spent her lunch hour reading stories to ailing children. She was a saint. A lying, conniving, scheming saint.

At least if we had a Barry he'd be mine. What if Dr. Henderson took one look at my overheated, sickly sperm and decided to replace it with some of his own? Would I be able to tell myself that it was God's work? Would my love for Julia be strong enough that I could adopt her happiness? I doubted it. I doubted it very much.

*But look at the other side of the ledger*, I thought, kicking away the duvet because I was hot. Julia and I might have twins. Or triplets. Or more. The Puregon Julia had been taking increased her normal production of follicles from one to six. The chances for having more than one baby were therefore higher. It reminded me of an *Oprah* show I'd seen where all the parents from one town had given birth to quadruplets. Oprah joked about the water supply, but now I knew it had nothing to do with water. The parents had been brought on the show to be celebrated, but even on national television, with all that makeup and goodwill, they looked tired and harassed and a little guilty. They'd gone from having no babies to having far too many.

I had to stay positive. It might all work out. And then what? Would I be the perfect father to a perfect child? Could I keep up with Julia's love? Could anybody?

# Destiny

THE FIRST STORK I'd ever made was for Mia, who'd placed it above an empty crib, in happy expectation of her unborn child. The bird was still there, dangling no longer over a crib, but over a bed and shelves.

Patrick was celebrating his fourth year of existence. He had carrot-coloured hair, pudgy legs, and a raw, pink face that still appeared traumatized from its encounter with the birthing canal. He looked not unlike his father. Patrick was crying from too much excitement and the sense that he was both the centre of attention and the person everyone wished to ignore.

Patrick's actual birthday had fallen three days earlier, on a Wednesday, when children his own age had been brought to his house for cake and loot bags, accompanied by their parents, or at least their mothers, some of whom were here again tonight and doing their best to ignore Patrick's screams.

Mia was juggling her second child, Tyler, a ten-month old, while trying to soothe the birthday boy. "Roger," she called out, "can you please take the baby?" But Roger, in the midst of a tight scrum of men, was busy opening another bottle of wine. He ignored her.

Mia had called us a week ago. "Patrick is turning four on Wednesday," she'd told me. "I want you to come to the party." When I'd told her that Julia and I would have trouble getting away from work in time for afternoon cake, Mia replied, "Oh not *that* party, that's for people who have children."

I'd flinched, hearing it put that way. Julia and I had been invited to the grown-up party, the one on Saturday night, where very un-grown-up people like us could come and enjoy themselves.

Mia and Julia had known each other since high school, but there'd been a falling off in the last few years. She and Roger no longer came over for dinner quite as often as they used to and we hardly ever visited them, even though they'd moved into a new home, bought, they said, to accommodate their growing family. Like her new house, which was regal and heavy-set as if built for war, ready to be shuttered and deployed for defensive purposes, there was something a bit too solid about Mia, as if she'd been built for potential opposition. And children were her weapons.

Mia, ignored by her husband, turned to Julia, who was standing beside her. "You can't imagine," I heard her say, "what having children does. Your life ceases to be your own."

Mia set Tyler down on the floor near a pile of brightly coloured toys and took a shallow sip of her wine, just enough, I thought, to confirm to everyone that she wasn't the sort of

mother who believed all life must cease with the bi
child. I saw her graze Roger with an angry look.

"It's so hard to balance. Work. Family." Mia weighted the air with wineglass and upturned hand.

It was an outcome Julia could only hope to look forward to and she stared, mesmerized by Mia's hands that rose and fell in opposition to each other like a grocer's scale seeking equilibrium.

Julia's wineglass was filled with innocuous sparkling water, in an attempt not to disrupt or in any way displease the fertility gods. It had been two weeks since her insemination, and her period, which until recently I'd known very little about but now knew was regulated like a Swiss clock, was more than three days late.

Egged on by Patrick, Tyler, too, started to cry.

"I'll take him," Julia said and I watched her step toward the wailing infant, pluck him off the ground, and hoist him onto her hip, all in one gracefully fluid motion as if baby-lifting were an Olympic sport that she had been secretly practising for years.

"I love the way he smells," Julia said, inhaling. "Like sweet milk."

Julia hadn't wanted to come this evening. It must have been difficult for her, I thought, to drag herself over here and feel the weight of Tyler's presence in her arms, see Patrick graduate from being a toddler, knowing she hadn't been invited to the parents' party, parents who, I noticed, didn't pick Tyler up in *their* arms because they had children of their own.

Tyler began to squirm, his legs paddled the air like a duck.

Julia called out to me.

"Do you want him?" she asked.

I didn't.

Mia took the baby out of Julia's hands and walked him over to me. "Go on," she said, "he won't bite."

Without any of the fluid grace I'd observed in Julia, I tried to pin him against my hip. Panicked, Tyler began to scream for his mother.

"He's hungry," Mia said.

*He's hideous*, I thought.

Mia took him back into her arms and I remembered how in years past she would unleash her right breast and begin to feed baby Patrick with over-exaggerated tenderness as if he were a piece of Venetian glass and she was blowing hot air through her nipples, sculpting her then only child to perfection.

Roger approached, his eyes glazed from too many glasses of wine.

"It's time to feed the baby and put him to sleep," Mia said.

Roger offered a cursory nod but made no move to help. He'd lost his job in computers shortly before the birth of his first son – "a downturn," he'd laconically remarked – and, staring at four-year-old Patrick, I realized that without proof or reason I'd come to associate his child with his unemployment. He'd found odd jobs here and there, some that paid rather well, but nothing ever stuck.

"Let me show you something," he said, tugging on my shirt.

I followed him down the hallway, thankful to be taken away from his sons and our wives, and walked past the sleek kitchen, with its dimmed lights and polished appliances and then into a back room that, in startling contrast to the rest of the house, looked like a Victorian train carriage, resplendent with bordello-red wallpaper, high-backed velvet chairs, absurdly verdant potted plants, brass knick-knacks of every description, and three floor-standing ashtrays, one for each of the occupied chairs.

"This," Roger declared with pride, "is my smoking room."

"But you don't smoke."

"You do," replied Roger.

I glanced at the three men sitting in their high-backed chairs – prosperous-looking, content, like railway barons, I thought. But they weren't smoking. The air was clean; the black alabaster ashtrays gleamed.

"I'm afraid I've quit, Roger."

The news upset him. "What's wrong with everyone? Everyone's so uptight."

I shrugged.

The only thing out of place in Roger's faux Victorian train carriage was a stack of circuit boards, plugs, wires, and phone cords piled up on a tabletop near the far, draped window. The entire ensemble gave off a particular brand of uselessness, very male and sad and curiously touching. It was reminiscent of my father's office, with its piles of never-to-be-produced film scripts. This room, this red, idiotic choo-choo room, was Roger's river basement. He wanted something magical to happen in it, some great, meaningful party to explode around him, but this wasn't the time, the era, for those sorts of illusions; instead, he had a smoking room with no smoke.

"Why'd you all quit?" Roger asked, addressing the three men sitting in his chairs, none of whom bothered to look up. They weren't his friends anyway – they were, like me, the husbands of Mia's friends, all of them fathers and so all of them not like me. That put me on the outside and made me feel a bit like Roger. I couldn't watch him be ignored in his own home, in his own special room by men who didn't care for him.

"Let's go and get another drink," I said, steering him out of the room, but it wasn't any better in the kitchen, where Mia was busily talking to Julia and another woman.

"Roger didn't want children so soon," she was saying, speaking about him and for him, despite his being less than ten feet away from her. "He said we were in the middle of our careers, but I said, then when are we going to have them, at the end of our careers? You just manage. Luckily, things work out."

As he reached for a beer, I wasn't so sure that things were working out for Roger. He'd lost weight, he was drinking too much, and I remembered what Julia had told me, that Roger's sex drive had taken a dive after he'd lost his job. This last piece of information was something I'd rather not have known. It was more than likely Julia had told Mia about our fertility problems. They'd been friends for a long time, had shared a great many secrets and experiences together. Why not this one? Roger probably knew as well, and it occurred to me that the most intimate details men learn about one another come from the lips of their own wives.

I moved in on Julia, ready to drag her away from the party, but Mia was still talking.

"And, with Roger at home all the time, we save money on babysitting." I began to suspect that Mia, far from being obtuse, was choosing her words very carefully. "I think it's easier with two children," Mia continued. "They keep each other company."

Cruelty, I decided, could be the only explanation for Mia inviting us to her son's birthday party. Either that, or she'd simply not considered its effect on Julia. I thought it was cruelty.

After saying our goodbyes we headed for home, neither of us saying a word in the car.

Our street was treelined, with narrow, red-brick houses, most with peaked roof and attic. I opened the sunroof, looked up and saw stars twinkling above canopies of branches swollen with midsummer leaves. I wondered if, sometimes, my wife regretted marrying me.

Reaching for my keys at the front door, Julia slipped her arm in mine.

"Is everything okay?" She meant about us.

"I didn't like the way Mia kept talking about her children."

"She's just proud of them."

"Have you told her that we're trying to have a child?"

Julia pulled me closer and nodded.

"Then why would she go on, throwing them in your face like that? There must be a part of her that really hates you because only someone who hates you would do that."

"They're having problems."

I thought of Roger's unemployment, his strange smoking room, and his sadness.

"We all have our problems," I said.

In some ways, Julia was very naive about people. She never should have exposed herself the way she had; nothing good could come of it. I believed that the fewer who knew about our affairs, the better. I turned to Julia, who was standing at the front door waiting for me to open it. Before I could take out the keys, she whispered in the shadowy darkness, "I had my period last night," and began to cry.

# Sweeping Away the Dust

AFTER JULIA TOLD ME she wasn't pregnant, I began to notice back-to-school advertisements. They were everywhere. In the newspaper, on television, billboards, shop fronts. It was like thousands of Mias pressing their babies against our bodies, asking us to hold them. Didn't they know better? Couldn't they sense our difficulties? Show some respect, I wanted to shout. But instead I just sat there, mute and tense in front of the television set, hoping that Julia didn't see what I saw and knowing that she did because she was as mute and tense as I was.

In addition to the advertisements, a previously undetected army of prams, chubby babies, and pregnant mothers appeared to have invaded the city. I felt they'd come to haunt us, like ghosts; but, in time, it was Julia and I who became the ghosts, bodiless somehow because of our failure to procreate. I found myself talking a little faster whenever we floated past one of these obstacles, in some pathetic attempt to divert Julia's attention; sometimes, it was Julia who sped up her words, speaking rapidly while we passed the impossibly blue eyes of an infant, its unfocused gaze almost hurtful in its dismissal of us.

Julia took to our bed. Whenever I lay down beside her she moulded herself to my body, turning away only when the heat between us grew uncomfortable. She wanted me next to her – if I tried to crawl out of bed she'd reach out for me, even when asleep.

"I think I'm sinking," she said to me three days later, when the sun was shining but shades remained drawn.

"You're resting. Don't be so hard on yourself."

The fertility clinic prescribed a one month on, one month off program, to allow their customers' bodies time to rest and repair themselves. Julia found the enforced inactivity almost as painful as her initial failure to become pregnant. "I'm not resting, I'm waiting," she said. "You wait to see the doctor, you wait to take the drugs, you wait while you're on the drugs, you wait and hope, but you don't allow yourself to hope too much. I just want to get on with it."

"You think it will work next time?"

"Don't you?"

It wasn't my nature to be optimistic; it wasn't my role. "Of course I do," I responded.

"You're right about needing rest. I feel exhausted. Everything just feels so unnatural."

"Sometimes we have to do something unnatural to arrive at the most natural thing in the world."

What I said sounded true and accurate and absurd and meaningless. I was trying to support and bolster Julia in her time of need. All I could think was how contrived it felt, as if I were a bad actor reading cue cards written in Julia's handwriting.

These feelings didn't leave me even after Julia lifted herself out of bed, stripping off the stale sheets like unhappy thoughts, and returned to her normal routine. By week's end, she'd resumed her work with the pedophilic CEO. He was reluctant, she said, to talk openly about what he euphemistically referred to as "the incident," but Julia insisted it was better to feed the press information and be out in front of a story rather than lag reluctantly behind it.

Julia described her work as a game: "A puzzle that needs to be solved. And I'm good at solving puzzles." Julia had a job to do and she did it with pride and an added touch of perfection. I admired her cool professionalism and the voiding of personal sentiment that came with it – her own opinion of the CEO, she said, shouldn't be allowed to interfere with her work; she found discussions of moral accountability sophomoric and impractical.

And Julia's interest in her work got her out of bed, and kept her away from that other, more personal puzzle, with its moving parts and ever more mysterious rules. She began to walk past baby carriages and pregnant females as if they really *were* ghosts, apparitions that no longer had the power to haunt her.

Summer deepened and the colour of the sky faded to a sun-bleached white. The heat slowed the city down, muffled noise, made time crawl. Under its narcotic effect, Julia's return to the clinic went largely unmentioned. She bicycled off and took her drugs and slowly her face began to swell and ripen. Julia pressed down on her swollen cheeks with open palms and squinted at herself in the mirror.

"They warned me about this."

"It's probably the heat."

"My boobs are sore. So are my ankles. It's like I'm pregnant." She laughed at the idea. "They say it's because of water retention, but I didn't put on any extra weight last time." There was just a hint of hope in Julia's voice as if, maybe, possibly, the physical distortion she saw in the mirror might be a sign of future success.

Mia phoned frequently, not to ask after Julia but to recount her own troubles in such rambling detail that Julia found it difficult to interject even a few words of sympathy: "I know how hard it must be for both of you . . . I'm sure he's going to find another job . . . Yes, I know a lot of work is getting outsourced . . . No, it isn't good that he's crying all the time."

Poor Roger, I thought, I'd be crying too if I was married to Mia, without a job, sitting at home, taking care of two kids. Mia was greedy; she took from Julia and offered nothing in return. Or so I thought until Julia's brother, Barry, came for a visit and I was reminded how comforting Julia found his needs and how giving she was of her time.

They did not look alike, brother and sister. Julia's hair was blonde; Barry's a muddy mixture of black and brown. Julia's skin was fresh and fair; Barry's a blotted, damp layer that wrapped itself around him like a paper towel. But something – a genetic shadow – stalked both of them, hovered behind the eyes, wafted over their lips and limbs. And they were both on drugs now. The way both their faces looked puffed and bloated heightened the unwelcome resemblance.

Barry carried a knapsack loaded with chips, video games, Coke, and the apples Mrs. Riddell insisted he take along but knew he'd never eat.

Barry's parents offered all the material comforts – the best special-education schooling, sports equipment, Xboxes, Gameboys, CDs – all of it a great showering of neglect. Taking care of Barry was what Julia did. Which was why, when visiting, he'd punch me a little too hard in the shoulder and why, though Julia insisted he was just playing, I'd punch him back when she wasn't looking. We were rivals.

Barry had his obsessions, some normal, others less so. He liked talking about cars but also, with equal passion, the surface pavement they ran upon. The best tar in the world, he said, was made in Germany. Another interest of his: the accumulation of airline points. In the living room he said, "American Express has three new cards, normal, gold, and platinum, and they get you points when you use them. The best one is platinum because it gets you more points. You can use it for other things, but gold is almost as good."

"What colour is gold?" Julia asked.

"Yellow."

"And do you know why people like it so much?"

"Yeah."

"Because it lasts forever. You could give a piece of gold to your children and they could give it to their children and they to theirs and it would look exactly the same as when you first held it in your own hand."

But Barry wanted to talk about airline points.

Sitting there, listening, I began to gain a better understanding of why the Riddells stuffed their child's mouth with cookies and chips and Coke and let him watch hours of television. Even Julia, with all her good patience, eventually stood up and, without formal announcement, walked away, leaving me alone with Barry, as if it were a test, something I owed her as her husband, and myself as a human being.

"What airline do you like best?" I interrupted.

"Air Canada."

"Why?"

Barry began talking about forest fires, then sea urchins, and when I joined in he looked bored and slightly worried and quickly moved on to another topic. The only way to participate, I saw, was to enter the conversation obliquely, as Julia had done, by asking Barry questions, then answering them for him: "Have you ever eaten a sea urchin?" "Yeah." "They're soft inside and you eat it raw. What else can you eat raw?"

But Barry wasn't interested in what else he could eat that was raw and shouted for his sister. "Julia!"

Afterwards, when Julia and I were in bed and she thanked me for my help, I imagined how it must have been for her, growing up with his insistent, needful love. High-school friends like Mia didn't have retarded brothers; they wouldn't have known what it was like to be so depended on.

"You're very patient with Barry," I said.

Julia had just finished applying self-tanning lotion over her entire body – it was too hot outside to get the real thing – and was reclining over several towels, naked and stiff as if she was posing for a painting, to avoid staining the sheets.

"I've seen what people are like when they're around him, the way they pretend to be nice but can't even look at him. You don't pretend."

"You're right. I've never pretended to be nice to him."

Julia smiled. "I mean that you've never pretended he's normal. You're honest with him. That's the point. My parents have never really known what to do with him. From the moment he was born, they decided to treat him as if he was no different from anyone else, which I used to think was a good thing. But he's not like everyone else, is he."

"No, he isn't."

"So I was the one who took care of him, because I was the one who was honest."

"In some way you took care of your parents too," I pointed out.

Julia's declaration of honesty was somewhat comprised by the half-bottle of fake tan she'd smothered over her body. For Julia, painted toenails, an eyelash tint, or a fake tan signified the vanquishing of some inner darkness. I took all her body brightenings as signs of trouble, including the orangey paste now drying on her skin. Camouflage for the awkward weight gain induced by the fertility drugs and her return to the clinic.

Later, when the lights were out, I reached for her hand. "You've never blamed me."

Julia knew what I meant. She took a breath, loud enough for me to hear her.

"Would you have blamed me?" she asked.

"Yes, maybe. I'm not a saint. Neither are you."

"I never said I was."

"Maybe you should just admit that you blame me."

"I don't."

"You don't admit it or you don't blame me?"

Julia pulled off the sheets and got out of the bed. She was weirdly, glowingly brown. "I can't do this right now. I can't have a conversation about your insecurities. It's not about you."

"Isn't it always about me?"

"You think this is funny?"

"Not really."

"Why are you doing this? You've got to know how I'm feeling." Julia paused, as if to consider that I might not, in fact, have a clue. "I'm doing all this for us, for our future, and you can't let go of your selfish need for attention, even for one second."

"I'm the selfish one?" I said, my voice rising. "Me? You're the one who wanted to do this, to drag our lives into this mess. You walk around with this aura of disappointment all the time. Do you know what that's like for me? I never even noticed babies before. They didn't exist. But now they're everywhere, like dust in the air. You're this sad light that illuminates it all. You're the one that makes me see what I'm breathing in."

"And I hope you choke on it."

With that, Julia was gone down the stairs. The spare bedroom, the room that would hold our baby if we were ever to have a baby to hold, was right next door, too intimately close and too full of unmet promise for a proper escape. No, she would sleep on the couch tonight. Wasn't it typical of her, I thought, that she would punish me by letting me sleep in our bed.

# Making Birds

LIPS. BEE-STUNG, PROTRUSIVE, PROVOCATIVE. They belonged to a brown-haired, twenty-three-year-old mother of two who sat in front of me on the small wooden chair I'd provided. Her low-rise jeans had a gold zipper that, without buttonhole or belt, showed no demonstrable reason for staying closed. She had very pale skin and wore running shoes with laces that said PINKPINKPINK.

Hans had brought Tamara in for a job interview, which was fine except that I didn't have a job to interview for. He'd given me no warning, had just walked into the bird factory with an out-of-work single mother – and now he was watching me, waiting to see what I would do.

The three of us sat in the bird assembly room. It was here that the wings of each specimen – seagull, eagle, stork, and the occasional flying fish – were attached to their bodies.

Sometimes Hans, because he was bored and a bastard, liked to mix them up, dangling his tormented cross-breeds above my office desk. It was an outlet of sorts for his hostility, so I never complained. This room was also the place where we ate our lunch, made coffee, and held job interviews for non-existent jobs.

"The problem," I said, "is that I don't need anybody right now."

"She has skills," insisted Hans.

"I'm sure she does."

A certain tension hung in the air. Tamara, looking unsure of its exact origin and uninterested in finding out, crossed her legs and said, "The flag of Dominica has a bird on it."

Hans and I stared at her, mystified.

"I know where Dominica is," she protested, misinterpreting our silence. "I lived there, in Calibishie, with Dee. When I was pregnant with my second, Dee said we could make some money if we bought some windsurfers and rented them out. Like *that* worked. Anyway, there's a parrot on the flag. I painted them on the sails, so it kind of makes sense that I'm here, right? Hans said you could pay me under the table."

Hans nodded solemnly. "It is as if fate has brought you to the bird factory."

*Bastard*, I thought.

Hans, I was sure, had brought Tamara as revenge – for hiring him to work on birds, for being his boss, for just disliking me. He'd ambushed me with full-lipped Tamara because he knew as well as I did she was hopeless. It was a little game with him, bringing her here, a way to break up the day and amuse himself. I was about to tell Tamara once again that I didn't have a job opening, when Philip, who was in the next room affixing weights to bird wings, called out, "We could use an extra pair of hands." He glanced up from a wingtip and stole a look at Tamara. It was a hungry look, as if she were the ultimate jumbo bird, the one he'd waited all his life to clamp his weights on.

Philip's sudden collusion with Hans was unexpected and unappreciated. "No," I said, "we don't need another pair of hands."

Until this moment, Philip had always done what was best for the bird factory. No longer. For the sake of having Tamara around, he would abandon his principles and side with the man who called him Lurch. Hans was delighted by the opportunity Philip had handed him.

"But you always say how not enough work is being done," Hans said.

"I'm always saying that not enough work is being done by *you*. I don't need anybody else."

Annoyed, I stood up, on the pretense of fetching some cold drinks from the vending machine outside, unhappy with myself for not immediately putting an end to our meeting. Despite the fact we'd been talking about her, Tamara sat in her chair, staring down at her shoes as if, after her initial burst about Dominica, she'd turned herself off to conserve energy. Looking at her more closely, I noticed that her short-cut shirt revealed her belly button, which was an "outy," and felt that Tamara might be the sort of person who had some minor deformity, like double-jointed toes or a fading scar around her kneecap, the result of old surgery. The kind of thing she might affectionately point to if we were in bed together.

No woman had ever worked at the bird factory; no woman had ever applied. Tamara was clearly a disaster, with two children, no husband, and, as yet, no job. I was determined not to offer her one. Yet it occurred to me that having her around might make a good change from the pervasive, slightly depressive male aura of the place. She'd already made Philip perk up.

The heat outside was intense, a smothering yellow heat that hung over the city like a thick blanket. At first the high temperature had been welcomed with open windows and bared skin, but now it was hated, even feared. Houses were shut against it, air conditioners thrummed, and Hans had complained bitterly that the bird factory was too hot and that I was letting him sweat to save a few dollars. It wasn't true, of course, but even with the air conditioner constantly on, the heat both inside and out was withering.

The vending machine was located directly across from the Changs' warehouse. Mr. Chang was standing beside the open delivery door, awaiting yet another shipment of condom-wrapped lamps, his hair plastered to his sweating forehead. Mrs. Chang, behind him, waved at me. I waved back. Mr. Chang, thinking I'd initiated the greeting, offered a distracted nod. He had lamps on his mind and nothing else.

In a way it seemed strange that Julia and I, married, hoping to have children and spend the rest of our lives together, headed off every day, in separate directions, leading separate lives. The Changs were allies in the truer, perhaps more ancient sense. They shared a business together, were bound by money and skill and mutual struggle. What did they make of couples like Julia and me who walked away from each other every morning? Maybe our actions led to the sort of unnatural problems we were now having. Or maybe it led to Tamara, alone with two children, needing this shitty job.

Over the years I'd learned a few things about owning a business, the primary lesson being that one should never let compassion dictate decisions. It wasn't necessary to be an ogre, just a boss who didn't treat his employees like his friends. In the beginning I'd wanted everyone to like me, to let them know I wasn't really the sort of person who demanded they get out of bed early and work late. But that, to my initial discomfort and eventual acceptance, was exactly who I was. I no longer drove employees home, bought them lunch, or advanced them money except, of course, when I drove them home, bought them lunch, and advanced them money. Still, I was not going to give Tamara a job.

When I returned to the factory, I found that everyone had removed themselves to the paint room or, as Hans called it, the abattoir. Four clotheslines were strung from one end to the other, pegged not with shirts or pants but bird bodies and wings, which Tamara, in canary-yellow overalls, was busy dipping in paint. Their bodies dripped white blood onto the floor.

"What's going on?"

Philip and Hans were both hovering over their protégée, offering encouraging smiles.

"She is very good at this," Hans said. The yellow overalls Tamara was wearing were his. He'd obviously initiated this little teaching session, but Philip, made courageous by his bird knowledge, vigorously nodded in agreement. "Can we keep her?" Hans asked, as if she were a pet.

I still had the drinks in my hand and made my way down one of the rows, careful not to touch the wet, dripping skins.

Passing a can of Sprite to Tamara, I stunned myself by offering her a job.

"Just one day a week," I said. "Maybe more in late October when we start making birds for the Christmas season."

"Cool," her lips said. Tamara seemed to take her drink for the same reason she took the job, because it was offered rather than needed, which I knew it was. As for Philip, he could barely contain his excitement. "I'll show her the ropes," he blurted. He held out an unpainted bird body by the tip of its beak and attempted to show her the run of the grain by gliding his hand down its smooth, sanded surface. Tamara feigned interest.

"Sometimes we make over a hundred birds a day," Philip said. The number obviously impressed Tamara because she turned to me and said, "Do you think I could take some birds home with me later? I promised my kids if I got the job I'd bring some home. They told me we'd have to put screens on our windows so they wouldn't fly away."

Tamara smiled proudly at this evidence of her children's imagination. It was here, I suppose, that some polite praise would have been appropriate, but I wasn't in the mood to discuss the wonders of children with her, particularly since she'd asked for free stuff within an hour of reaching the bird factory.

"Why don't we make the birds from scratch," Philip eagerly suggested, leading her away to the cutting room. Moments later, I heard the whir of the band saw, then the sharp whine as the metal teeth bit into the wood.

I returned to my office and decided to call Julia.

"Do you want to see a movie later?" I asked.

"Can't. I'm working late tonight," she said.

"We could catch something at nine-thirty."

"No, I'm tired. I just want to go home and crash. Do you mind?"

I lingered on the phone, wanting to tell her about Tamara, about Hans and how he'd manipulated me, but I heard her begin tapping at her computer, as busy and important as ever, and decided not to. Julia would never have hired Tamara. She would have sent her packing, Hans too probably. Especially Hans.

"I guess I'll pick up something to eat on the way home."

"Okay. See you," Julia said absent-mindedly and hung up the phone.

"Talking to your wife?" It was Hans. He'd been standing behind me, listening. "You know, you are like a barnacle that has attached itself to a beautiful ship and slowed her down. If your wife knew what was good for her, she would scrape you off and sail away."

"Fuck off, Hans."

With paint-stained fingers, he plucked a cigarette out of his pocket, stuck it in his mouth, lit it, pulled the smoke into his lungs, then let it seep out his nostrils. He never took his eyes off me.

"Want one?"

"I quit."

"Aren't you good," he said. "Clean lungs, clean mind, yes?"

"What do you want?"

"I did not expect you would hire her. You are a very weak man." Once more, Hans offered me a cigarette, which again I refused. "You will see that working at the bird factory is far worse for your health than chain-smoking, which my uncle died of, one last cough while he was sitting in his chair and *pftt* his lungs were in his lap."

"That's a really great story, Hans."

Hans leaned in and whispered slyly, "She is attractive."

"So what?"

"Why did you hire her?"

"I don't know. Maybe I wanted to do a good thing."

Hans shook his head.

"Too late," he said.

# Getting Involved

A SHALLOW, IMPASSABLE GASH ran down the centre of the road, backing up traffic for two city blocks on either side. Construction crews – pockets of five or six men in hardhats and reflective safety vests – were ripping out decayed streetcar tracks, indifferent to the morning rush-hour exhaust that swirled impatiently around them. I looked at the dashboard clock: 8:38. The sample time, recorded from the bedroom clock, was set at 8:20. In ten minutes or so my sperm would be dead.

Julia rested in the passenger seat, chair deeply reclined, reading a magazine, oblivious to the danger. She wasn't wearing a seat belt, which annoyed me.

"Put your seat belt on."

"But we're not moving." Julia continued to read her magazine.

"Just put it on. I could get a ticket!"

I leaned over, grabbed the shoulder strap, pulled it over her body, and heard the satisfying *snap* as I pressed the metal tongue into its holster. *Would they all die?* Surely not every single one of them. The clinic told us thirty minutes because they knew it would take us forty, maybe forty-five minutes. On the other hand, it really was extraordinary they could live for even a few seconds out in the open. Before the advent of fertility clinics and the need to transport sperm along city roads, what would have been the point?

It had been two months since our last, unsuccessful attempt. Julia hadn't been sure she wanted me to come with her this morning. A part of her must have appreciated the company, must have known, as I'd wanted her to know, that my presence here was a show of support, that I was part of the team and accountable. But Julia's behaviour these past weeks, ever since she'd started periodically sleeping on the couch, made me feel like an intruder in her important personal affairs.

We'd discussed our problems – that is to say, I had apologized for my outburst – and come to terms with the inevitable tensions one would experience under the conditions we found ourselves in, yet occasionally Julia still removed herself from our bedroom. Even when I woke up and found her sleeping beside me, there was often a crumpled sheet and pillow on the couch when I came down for breakfast, raw proof where she'd spent the night.

At first Julia said it was because she found it cooler downstairs, but when the heat wave broke, chased away by a lightning storm, she switched excuses and said it was because of her sinuses. Sometimes, when I awoke at night and found our bed empty, I'd go downstairs and watch her sleeping, her mouth open like a dead fish.

I honked the horn.

Not twenty feet away, off to my right, stretched a blissfully empty street. Take it one block, turn south, drive three more blocks, then cut back and maybe I'd make it to the clinic on time.

Julia put down her magazine and laid a comforting hand on my knee.

"Luke, I'm not in labour."

I pointed to the time displayed on the dashboard. "It's getting late."

"We have time. I've done this before, remember? Everything is going to be all right provided you don't kill us on the way there."

Tucked beneath the rim of Julia's underwear was the vial. *Good place*, I thought. Warm, close to future action, appropriately symbolic. As long as my sperm showed up within half an hour, the rest of me could be left behind. Last time she'd produced six follicles. This time, according to the doctor, she'd produced four, which disappointed her, but it was still better than just the single follicle she'd normally have had. In essence, Julia was increasing her own fertility to compensate for mine.

"Don't worry," Julia said, tapping the blue vial top with her fingertips. "They're happy."

"How do you know?"

"I just do."

There was a pause. She was remarkably Zen, I thought. Very self-contained and aloof. It bothered me.

"I'm hungry," I said.

"You just had a large breakfast. How can you be hungry?"

"I don't know, I just am. Aren't you?"

Julia, who hadn't had anything to eat this morning, shook her head. She wasn't much interested in the conversation, was even, by the tight little wag of her head, slightly hostile. After all, what were my needs compared to the billions tucked against her body, waiting for their chance? Julia hadn't made me breakfast in bed this morning. There'd been no ceremony with eggs and bacon. Instead, I'd gone downstairs and made my own breakfast before returning to the bedroom.

The time on the dashboard read 8:44.

The air outside was impure. I could taste the particles of pulverized concrete emanating from the ever-widening gash in the road and changed the vent setting from External to Internal. We were in Julia's car. According to the brochure, which Julia had never read but I'd diligently studied as if the cure for cancer might be found within its glossy pages, the vehicle contained two active carbon filters. They worked in tandem, and filtered out the unwanted parts of the world. Dr. Henderson had spoken of sperm baths and I, in a case of over-anxious literalism, envisioned my semen being dunked and scrubbed clean, each with a wide sea-monkey smile on its face. But in point of fact a sperm bath was more likely allied to the technology in this car: the unwanted particles, the deformed, the unbalanced, the ones that swam backward when they should have gone forward, were to be filtered out.

"Break!" Julia pointed to a small gap that had opened up between our car and the clear street to our right. "Take it," she urged. "Take it!"

Startled by her sudden anxiety, I sped off down the road.

Julia got off at the curb. It was agreed she should get out first. I would park the car and meet her at the clinic; but before I put the car in drive, Julia's brisk stride toward the office tower caught my attention. I sensed she wanted to run. Around her, men and women dressed for work headed toward the same set of doors, coffee cups and briefcases in hand, most with expressions of nervous anticipation. In addition to cups of coffee and briefcases, how many had vials of sperm tucked beneath their clothes? *You can never really tell what people are up to*, I thought.

"It's not very personal, is it?" Julia whispered when I joined her in the waiting room. She'd reserved the seat next to her with her purse, which she'd pulled off as soon as she spotted my approach. Unlike the other times I'd been here, the waiting room was full.

"Morning rush hour?"

"Consultations are in the afternoon. This is the time they do the real work."

The room was filled with the surprisingly young and, in some cases, the surprisingly old. They wore head scarves, shawls, saris, baseball caps; it was like an airport in here – the sperm of a hundred nationalities idling on the tarmac, waiting for takeoff.

Julia sighed and rested her head on my shoulder. It felt heavy and hot. I stroked her hair. Why did I always think Julia was stronger than she was? For convenience sake, I decided; it was easier for me to think of her that way. If she needed *my* help, then what hope did we possibly have?

Julia's name was called.

"Wish me luck," she said, and for the first time I was happy to be here, happy Julia wasn't alone in this place.

"Good luck," I said.

After her departure, I leafed through a sporting magazine. It was full of men playing games from half a year ago. I put it down. Most of the patients were couples, but a few women sat by themselves. They looked vulnerable. One of the women, dressed in a blue business suit, made me think of Julia. How many times had she, like Julia, been here alone? She had long legs, elegantly crossed at the calves. I found her attractive and wondered what her husband looked like and if it was her fault or his that she was here. The woman caught my eye. I looked away. And then I looked up.

I must have seen it as I'd walked in because it was dangling down in front of the window, and yet I'd failed to notice it. But there it was, a giant stork, put there by the clinic as a symbol of hope, suspended in air.

Julia must have brought a bird to one of her routine check-ups. My wife was a believer in gifts, for the joy they brought and the loyalty they conferred. She'd littered the world with her little business presents: autographed baseballs for her Japanese clients; virginally pure maple syrup for the Germans; hockey jerseys for everyone. In return, she'd received wooden clocks, Geisha scarves, pens, and a great number of business contracts. She'd presented Dr. Henderson with a bird for only one reason – to get something back in return.

I stared at the bird. I looked into its eyes. Though I'd experimented with stick-on decals and stamps, I'd found that nothing replaced the glossy black drop of paint that dripped off the edge of a brush. No matter how hard reason cautioned, I found it impossible not to believe that somewhere, deep in the grain, there was life; a dim watt of consciousness peering back at me.

I'd learned over the years that each bird said something about its maker. Hans placed the eye either too far forward, so that they looked mean-spirited, or too far back, so that they looked docile and stupid, or he placed one eye lower than the other, to make them look retarded, a sort of flying Barry. Philip's birds, in contrast, had an appealing competence about them, but in their similarity to one another you noticed, if you singled out any one bird for further inspection, a certain despondency, as if they knew they didn't warrant the extra attention.

This bird was different. The eyes weren't perfect round dollops of paint, but slanted and slightly off centre; yet this wasn't the work of Hans, whose skills with a brush ensured that any mistakes were purposeful. This must have been Tamara's bird. She'd only come into the factory to string wings to bodies, so how, I wondered, could this be hers? And then I remembered: Philip and Tamara, cheek by cheek, his hand gliding over the wood grain. He must have taken her right through the process, and Julia had somehow brought one of her storks to the fertility clinic.

When Julia returned I expected her to be pale or glowing, different in some detectable way, but she wasn't.

"Let's go," she said.

I bent my head back and looked up at the ceiling. Julia, noticing, said, "I asked Philip to send one to my office. If you're angry with me, I don't want to hear it." She looked at me with those steady eyes. *You can't paint eyes like that*, I thought. "I brought a bird to the clinic to make them remember me. Now the nurses know my name. Every little bit helps."

My Julia. Hustling the angle, getting things done.

We walked to the elevator and waited for the doors to open.

"It's kind of strange you didn't ask me."

"Is it?" Julia punched the Down button.

Strange or not, there was something appropriate about Tamara's stork ending up in a fertility clinic: I was lazy, Hans was gay, and Philip was chronically single. Tamara had two children. Julia had none.

I still hadn't told Julia about my new hire. I'd meant to – I had nothing to hide – but I hadn't. Because I'd forgotten, because time had gone by, because if I told her now I would have to state it in an offhand way that would sound like I did, in fact, have something to hide. It didn't feel altogether right that Julia had carried Tamara's bird into the fertility clinic.

"If you had asked me and not Philip, I would have brought a better bird."

"Why? What's wrong with this one?"

The elevator arrived. Another couple from the fertility clinic followed behind us as we stepped inside. The husband instinctively reached out for the ground-floor button even though it was already illuminated, and I suddenly decided that I disliked the sort of person who did that. The glint of his wedding band caught my attention, shiny and polished like new money.

I whispered to Julia, "You haven't told me. How did everything go?"

Julia nodded and then, only when we reached the main lobby, said, "It'll work or it won't."

The couple in the elevator was still behind us, as if they couldn't break free. I slowed down my pace and waited for them to pass.

"Do you want me to drive you back home?"

"No, I have a busy day at the office."

"Don't you need to lie down or something?"

Julia patted my arm and said she wanted to walk to work so she'd better get going. "Make me dinner?" she asked.

"Sure. I'll see you tonight." I felt awkward, standing in the lobby amongst the late stragglers rushing toward their office towers. We'd done so much already, I thought. It didn't seem imaginable the day had only just begun.

# Getting More Involved

I DECIDED TO LEAVE Julia's car in the parking lot. After she left for the office, I realized how long it had been since I'd walked the downtown streets, alone, in the morning. I felt suddenly light-headed, weightless, as if I could sprint down the street without breaking a sweat. Offices and shops were open for business. It all looked busy and important and, compared to where I'd just come from, wonderfully trivial.

In these first days of September, the cooling wind felt good on my skin, evaporating the sticky, unsettled feeling I had after our experience at the clinic. Events, like the seasons, had overtaken Julia and me, but the brisk fall wind reminded me that my father had started teaching again. Duncan always professed a great love for the harsh extremes of the four seasons, but in truth he existed in just one climate, a sort of autumnal gloom, perpetuated in the basement and the dimly lit editing suites and repertory movie theatres he so loved to inhabit. And the gloom existed too at The Steak House restaurant, whose lacquered black door I now opened, in search of my father.

The restaurant was only a couple of blocks away from Ryerson University, where Duncan, despite his initial assertions that he would never step inside a classroom, taught film studies. He'd started teaching there shortly after the basement had flooded, when Ryerson was just a lowly polytechnic and his colleagues were marooned and embittered ex-movie directors from Eastern Europe. Duncan frequented The Steak House after his weekly History of Documentary Cinema course, which started at 8 a.m. and finished three hours later. The restaurant was like a darkened drinking lounge, which in many ways it was, making it difficult to properly see what one was eating. My mother had never liked it here. The sizzling hunks of meat, the French onion soup, the smell of beer and cheapish wine. If, as I suspected, my father's routine had remained unchanged, I'd find him sitting in one of the high-banked booths, sipping coffee.

I was coming to see, despite my reluctance, that life *was* change, a ceaseless reordering of things; witness Julia and me. Yet the restaurant seemed frozen in time – same brown-leathered banquettes, same diamond-patterned blue carpet, same wagon wheel and wine rack over the bar. The place hadn't altered since Duncan had first brought me here on my ninth birthday when my mother was gone. The restaurant had presented a wedge-shaped piece of chocolate cake, nine lit candles circling the rim. "Like a chain-link fence protecting an abandoned field," Duncan had said, plucking off some of the candles so he could take a bite. "And we're in the field."

Macedonian George, who'd brought me the cake all those years ago, recognized me and pointed toward the corner of the L-shaped restaurant. It was just past eleven and, having felt hungry all morning, I ordered a New York strip loin and carried on past the empty booths until I saw my father, his head bent down, looking into his coffee cup. The restaurant was nearly deserted, but he was here because this was Thursday morning. Despite expansion, renovations, changes of presidents and department heads, my father's Thursday-morning schedule had never altered. I'd never been sure if this was an indication of his status or bureaucratic indifference.

Duncan started teaching after his failure with *Angry Voices* could no longer be ignored. Course descriptions for his classes read: *The exact content of the course will vary according to student interests and abilities*. Students watched films and wrote earnest, over-reaching papers, which my father often disparaged and very occasionally praised.

As time went on, his students, if they'd even vaguely heard of Duncan Gray, had certainly not seen his films. Also, film and television had become big business to the city of Toronto. Ryerson set up and expanded its program, adding courses like Movie Marketing and Commercial Writing to its calendar. All of which explained, according to Duncan, why there were so many good-looking women walking down the hallways. It was, he said, all very male in the old days – men who wore scruffy jeans and drank coffee out of plain, white Styrofoam cups and talked shop. Now, many of the men were better dressed than the women. BMWs, even a Jag or two, could be found in the student parking lot.

All this baffled my father. Duncan would complain that former students of his, students who had previously wanted to be film directors or DOPs, were now making toothpaste ads or had become television producers. Many of them were cracking over a hundred thousand dollars a year. "They're doing as well as your mother," he'd petulantly joke. A part of him still couldn't understand why they didn't want to hang out in his basement, making waterfalls.

But the years passed and my father hung on teaching, and as I walked toward him I could, if not admire, at least appreciate his sheer staying power.

"Hi, Dad."

My father snapped his head up. He looked frightened.

"I came to say hello," I said and because Duncan hadn't seen me until the last second and because I hadn't seen the young woman who was sitting opposite him, both of us were full of regret over my decision.

I stared at the woman. *Girl*, I corrected myself, she was a girl, a student, twenty, maybe twenty-one, long, reddish hair and an expression that conveyed a certain stubbornness and possible stupidity.

The girl's hands, which I now saw had been the source of my father's interest, were placed halfway across the table – no, not halfway, they'd crossed over the boundary of friendship and now were stuck, by my hostile gaze, in foreign territory.

"I'm Luke Gray. And that's my father."

The girl retracted her hands, slowly, palms down like a scolded dog. "I think I should go," she said quietly, politely.

I sat down beside her, blocking her way out of the booth. "Are you my father's student?"

She nodded and said, "I had him last year," and, perhaps due to this regrettable phrasing, looked for a brief moment as if she was about to cry. My mouth felt parched. I noticed a glass of water on the table in front of her. "Do you mind?" I asked, taking a sip. I put the glass back down on the table.

"Have you watched *Angry Voices*?" I asked. Again, the girl nodded. "It's a film about the nineteen-seventies. And since you weren't born then, I can see how it might interest you as a matter of history."

I laughed coldly and stared at my father. There had never been much order to my father's face – it drooped in odd and inappropriate places – but, like iron filings, it was held in position, was patterned, around his magnetic, steel-grey eyes. They were the centre of him, the binding force that prevented everything else from falling away. They were avoiding me now.

"I'm going," the girl said.

I stood up to let her pass and my father darted to the edge of the booth, to help escort her out, but he never managed to lift himself off the seat. She left without looking at him. In the silence that followed, Macedonian George brought my starters of soup and iceberg salad that by custom I offered to my father, who wordlessly accepted the salad. He picked up a fork and stirred the dressing, an orangey paste that reminded me of Julia's self-tanning lotion. Eventually, he said, "She's pregnant."

Someone from the kitchen opened the back door to accept a delivery. I looked out into the bright day and blinked.

"Are you sure?"

"Just over three months. It's mine. I've tried to reason with her."

"Reason? It's a bit late for that, don't you think?"

I turned to examine the slight but noticeable depression her body had marked on the cushioned banquette. She hadn't fully left us. The woman – the girl – had been neither pretty nor ugly, I decided. She was just young, and that made her attractive, like Tamara.

"Didn't you use a condom?"

"No. It wasn't anything serious," he said, as if that explained it. "We just spent a few nights together at the end of last semester. Now she's going to have the baby because, get this, she's Catholic. She doesn't believe in abortion. Apparently, a Catholic girl who fucks university professors has certain moral principles to uphold."

"It might have been a good idea to inquire as to her religious sentiments before you started sleeping with her," I said. "What's her name?"

"Rosemary," Duncan said morosely.

I'd observed a certain stubbornness and stupidity in Rosemary, but in retrospect what I'd thought of as stubbornness may simply have been her principles; what I took to be stupidity was perhaps nothing less than the awkward manner in which her principles exerted themselves.

"Nowadays, people wear condoms to protect themselves against disease as much as pregnancy. Didn't you think of Emily? No, of course not."

Duncan tried to dismiss my concern with a wave of his hand, but he looked hollowed out by worry.

"Look at what all those years of condom wearing did for you?"

"What does that mean?"

"Maybe if you hadn't been so careful, you might have something to show for all that activity." Duncan sighed. "Your mother told me about your problems with Julia. You know how she can't keep away from bad news."

"It's not bad news," I said. "We're getting help. In fact, I've just come from the fertility clinic. Julia was inseminated this morning."

"I see the irony," said Duncan.

My steak arrived. I cut open my potato and slathered it with butter. Duncan watched it melt and breathed in the fragrant steam. Nothing robust entered his gullet any more; he didn't have the stomach for it. This had not, I noticed, prevented my father from putting on weight. He did not carry it proudly as some men do, with their drum-tight bellies and sagacious jowls, but submissively, as if he'd allowed the food to conquer him. He waited for me to take a bite of my steak. Then he said, "You have the same look on your face now as you did when you were a kid and found me with that woman in the basement. All that judgment, all that shock and hurt and anger. I can't stand it."

"I didn't *find* you in the basement. I caught you."

"What is it with your generation? I mean, that whole low, weird, vacant, infertile generation of yours, the one that slouches not toward Bethlehem but fertility clinics. You wear condoms to protect yourself against death instead of life. Everyone's so afraid to live! I tell you, I don't understand you or my students any more."

"You understand them well enough to get one of them pregnant. What are you going to tell Emily?"

"I'm not going to tell her anything."

"You don't think you can keep this a secret from her, do you?"

"Why, are you going to say anything?"

"Don't put me in the middle of this."

"You're in it already. You found me here."

"I *caught* you here."

Duncan stood up.

"I'm going now," he said, before realizing he hadn't paid his cheque.

"Don't worry about it," I said, but Duncan sat back down and waited for George to hand him the bill, which he signed with a flourish that did not match his mood, as if the pen had taken momentary possession of him.

"She liked my films," he said, just before leaving the table. "I think that's why I slept with her, because she liked my films."

I looked at him in astonishment.

"I know," he said, shrugging his shoulders. "But sometimes the most pathetic excuse is the right one."

# No Fault Insurance

DR. HENDERSON COUNSELLED FOR CALM.

"But how could I have killed off all his sperm? I'm his wife!"

"It was only a test and not a very meaningful one at that. I wouldn't put too much on it."

"Then why did you give it to me?"

"We're just trying to get as much information as we can."

"Because I can't get pregnant."

*Obviously*, I thought. Why else would we be here again? Disappointment had made her obtuse.

Julia had been having trouble sleeping ever since she'd discovered she wasn't pregnant again. After her first failure at the clinic, Julia had taken to her bed. This time, her anger and frustration kept her away from it. A week ago, Julia had gone around the house at two in the morning replacing all our lights with high-efficiency bulbs. When I'd gone downstairs to see what she was doing, she'd yelled at me about the electrical bill.

"You can get pregnant," said Dr. Henderson. "You just aren't pregnant right now. So, let's see where we are." He opened the manila folder that contained our case history. Where we were, of course, was nowhere, but I elected to sit in my chair and say nothing.

Dr. Henderson had been away at a conference in Tampa, and, in contrast to our own declining fortunes, had greeted us with the sort of overconfident health people who spend too much time on golf courses convey. His tan was glossy and obvious and, though genuine, looked as if it had been applied. And I was sure he'd dyed his hair, which was an unnatural shade of peacock black.

"My periods are irregular," Julia said.

Dr. Henderson lifted his fingers off the pages he was still studying, like flies temporarily disturbed, then settled them back down. "That's to be expected." There seemed to be a lot of things that "were to be expected" that I hadn't expected.

"Is it the effect of the drugs?"

"Yes."

"I'm usually so regular."

"Uh-huh."

Dr. Henderson continued to read the material before him: lab reports, doctors' notations, nurses' observations, most of it coloured purple, blue, or white depending upon which piece of triplicate had settled in his folder. In the silence my mind wandered to my father. I hadn't spoken with him again after our conversation at The Steak House. I'd had other things to worry about, and, if I was honest with myself, had tried to block the whole thing from my mind, especially when speaking to my mother, who peppered me with questions about Julia and the clinic without having the faintest clue that her own husband was about to become a father.

Duncan had probably used the past few weeks to continue lobbying for an abortion, though it was probably too late to do anything about it now. I wouldn't be surprised if, having failed to win his argument, he had, like me, just tried to block the whole thing from his mind. Pretend it wasn't happening.

"I just don't understand. How could every one of his sperm be dead?"

The clinic, perhaps out of need to show that it was doing *something* after our second failed insemination, had placed some sort of cap inside Julia's vagina and injected a dose of my sperm, then pulled the cap out and examined it under a microscope. The test results had not pleased Julia.

"You didn't kill all of them," the doctor assured.

But Julia wasn't placated. "Is this why we can't have any children? If there's a problem, you'd better tell us."

In the past six months, she'd had her tubes blown, her eggs examined, her sexual and medical history scrutinized, all in an attempt to search for any blockages, scarring, or other obstructions that might waylay my lazy, hindered sperm, and she'd passed every test, no matter how invasive and difficult. Until now. Julia, frustrated and sleep-deprived, demanded an explanation, perhaps as a way of claiming some sort of control over the situation.

Dr. Henderson did not like being spoken to this way. "Your body is reacting to Luke's sperm as if it were a foreign substance. It's a fairly common occurrence and doesn't prove one thing or the other because we inject the sperm past the cervix, where all the trouble is. Again, it's a rather meaningless test."

It seemed hardly possible, but it looked to me like the doctor had added even more baby pictures to his collection since our last visit to his office. Their swaddled bodies, pointed in my direction, amplified Dr. Henderson's next question to me, which was loud and curiously aggressive.

"Have you ever got anyone pregnant?"

I shook my head. "I always thought that was a good thing," I said.

Julia reached out for my hand and gave it a sympathetic squeeze.

In high school, a kid named David Higgins had got his girlfriend pregnant not once, but twice. Everyone thought he was an idiot, but most of us were still virgins so we were also filled with secret admiration.

I'd only had one close call. Six or seven years ago, a woman I'd dated for several months told me her period was late and we'd waited seven, maybe ten days, before she told me that everything was okay. Over the course of my entire sexual history, that was my only reproductive drama. I could barely remember it now; David Higgins had left a stronger impression on me.

"Have you been taking your supplements?"

I nodded.

"Smoking?"

Dr. Henderson popped an imaginary cigarette into his mouth and mockingly sucked in the air.

My head, only seconds ago bobbing up and down in eager affirmation, now swung back and forth in firm denial.

"Good."

Hans still liked to entice me with open packages, the upper flap unsealed, a cigarette coyly extended. No use reporting to Dr. Henderson – or Julia – of my occasional puffs on the drive to and from work. The deal I'd made with myself was that I'd only smoke during the off months, when Julia didn't need me. This last test, which required a sample of my sperm, had taken me by surprise and I was a little frightened by what Dr. Henderson might have detected through his microscope. Luckily, I didn't have anything to worry about.

"Your sperm count has improved. Along with motility. But it's still not where I'd like it to be."

"You mean it's still lazy?" asked Julia.

"The performance could be better."

"Perhaps a new set of tires might help," I said.

Dr. Henderson turned to stare out one of his corner windows, more, I thought, for the chance of catching his own reflection than to see what lay beyond it.

"Taking into account your present difficulties I think we should move into in vitro fertilization, which is a more complicated and expensive treatment." Dr. Henderson smiled solicitously.

"Why didn't we try that before? Is that our last chance?" Julia asked, panic in her voice.

"I'll tell you everything you need to know about the procedure. But first, I want you to attend a learning seminar we put on at the clinic. We'll talk after that."

Dr. Henderson gathered his notes and slipped them into the manila folder. He was tidying up for his next appointment – another infertile couple, another set of fears, another set of hopes.

"Have you been paying for everything with a credit card that gives you airline points? You can fly somewhere after the procedure. Helps to take the mind off things. If you haven't been, I suggest Bermuda." Dr. Henderson was enthusiastic about Bermuda. "It's a very pleasant island. Only a two-and-a-half-hour flight. Did you know that it has a higher standard of living than Switzerland?"

We shook our heads.

"No one pesters you on the beach. I hate it when people come up and try to sell you things. And it's safe. Do you play golf? No? Well, it's a great place to learn. They have beautiful courses."

Julia had other things on her mind. "I've been doing some research. Statistically, fertility clinics have about a fifty per cent success rate. I want you to tell me how you rate our situation."

"I know it's difficult," the doctor said, clearly sending us on our way.

I stood up. "Let's see what happens," I said to Julia, holding out my hand for her. She looked at it with undisguised contempt.

When we reached the hallway Julia broke for the washroom. I felt stupid standing there alone, a lurker. The hallway led to secret sections of the clinic. There were lots of doors, but only one was open. I could see several swivel chairs pushed back from a conference table as if the occupants had been called away by some emergency.

Just then Dr. Henderson exited his office and passed by with a furtive nod of his head that may or may not have contained a trace of sympathy for my solitary stance in his hallway.

Just as I began to think Julia might have snuck out and left me here, she came out of the bathroom and walked toward me.

I could tell she'd been crying because her eyes were puffy and she'd reapplied her mascara.

"Let's go," she said, without stopping.

We reached the waiting room, the only area of the clinic besides the doctor's office that I'd visited. It was almost empty at this time of the day, late afternoon, empty and without promise. Just a few people sat in the chairs, all of them women, magazines on their laps, their eyes focused beyond its glossy pages, to their shoes, to the floor. Maybe their thoughts drifted toward what they would have for supper. I imagined they thought of anything except what they really wanted.

"I don't want to come back here," said Julia.

"Where do you want to go then?"

"Somewhere else."

"We can't start over again," I said. "For better or worse, we know them and they know us."

"So we just go on with these people because it's easier than starting again? Since when did you get so attached to this place?"

"Julia, I'm not the enemy. I'm trying to get through this, just like you."

Unaware of what she was doing, Julia rubbed her belly. "Nothing's changed," she said.

Tears began to dampen her eyes, threatening to muddy her freshly applied mascara and whatever sympathy I had for her. I didn't want to comfort her; I *hated* her. My normally steady wife was starting to frighten me. I'd grown up with enough of other people's manias and I didn't need any more now. I'd married Julia to avoid that sort of thing.

"It's going to be all right," I pronounced, in an attempt to head off her tears.

"Is it?"

*Was it?*

"Yes."

Hovering over the reception desk was Tamara's bird, serene and untroubled, its outstretched wings catching the westerly light streaming through the windows. Julia looked up at it and said, "It's funny how much comfort your birds used to give me."

"And now?" I asked.

"They still do, but birds live in the clouds, Luke. People need to have their feet on the ground."

# A Pot of Gold

AS A TEENAGER, I never liked bringing girls home. Out of the need for privacy and an unwelcome compulsion, I'd take them downstairs to the renovated basement, where the door to the furnace room and my bird workshop was kept firmly shut. I'd make out with them over the ghost of my father's river, thinking that it was like doing it over someone's grave.

A similar thought must have occurred to my mother, who invariably attempted to befriend any girl I brought home. Not just befriend them, but console them, counsel them, warn them. She'd let them know that they could speak freely with her, and studiously fostered an atmosphere of understanding and openness that I felt incapable of competing with, because I was neither particularly insightful nor charitable toward the girls I brought down to the basement.

At some point or another, they would inevitably break free of my attempts to lose my virginity and ascend toward my mother. When I went up to fetch them, my presence provoked silence and a protective crook of my mother's shoulder as if warning me to stay away from her new-found charges.

I, son of Duncan, Lord of the Underworld.

My father, ignoring the girls that came and went, spent most of his time in his study, but I sometimes found him staring out of the living-room window at the renovations going on in our street, whispering, "I can't go on like this."

Plainly visible from the window, the house across the street was in the early stages of a massive makeover. The exterior paint, which the previous Portuguese owners had allowed to peel, had been stripped off and workmen were busy gutting the house. Duncan, whenever he spotted the new owners, would raise a fist at them from behind the window. "Fucking yuppies!"

It was my mother who'd sold them the house.

Our own house had undergone extensive renovations only the year before. Walls had been knocked down, a new kitchen assembled, upgraded floorboards and lighting installed. Everything had been remodelled except for my father's study, because Duncan had refused to have his brown walls repainted or his warped wooden window frames, propped open with unread film scripts during the summer, replaced or even repaired.

"You're not coming in here," he'd warned, standing at the doorway to his office when Emily brought the interior decorator to our house. His office was now more cluttered than ever, filled with the chairs and lamps and side tables my mother had targeted for disposal.

As a consequence, my father's study was not a pleasant place to visit. There was nothing romantic about the past my father had chosen to preserve, and nothing of value either except for a small wooden box that sat on the bottom shelf. The box came from Turkey, bought on a trip my parents had made before I'd been born. But its origin was not what made it valuable, at least not to me. It was in that box that Duncan stored his ever-plentiful plastic baggies of British Columbian weed. At least I thought it was British Columbian. That's what Nicola told me, and she seemed to know everything about drugs. When adults like our parents smoked up they smoked the best, and the best, she insisted, came from the West Coast.

Wherever it came from, Nicola Green liked it. And I liked Nicola Green. It wasn't just what she knew about drugs. Nicola had the gift of being able to definitively evaluate just about everything, including people. She knew where people belonged, whom they belonged with, what music they liked to listen to, if they were funny, or sad, or insane. She didn't seem to care one way or the other, or rather she didn't seem to have any preferences, and that made her unlike anyone I knew.

She also looked unlike anyone I knew. The girls I usually brought back to the basement wore jeans and running shoes. They might be cute or pretty, but compared to Nicola they were hopeless. She wore fur coats, had a mane of blonde hair, and a slight bump on the bridge of her nose that should have been a detraction but instead made her look imperious. She owned an enormous collection of expensive handbags and cloaked her bed in satin sheets. She told me that everything in life, including herself, was disposable. "We're throwaways," she said.

Nicola lived with her mother in a townhouse with a vaguely Japanese feeling to it. The furniture was low to the ground, the plants looked artificial but were not, and black-and-white photos of Nicola's mother, a few years younger than she was now, hung on the walls. I often thought they'd been put there to keep her daughter company.

"She's on another trip," Nicola would tell me, opening the door to her empty house. Those trips took her mother skiing and sunbathing and yachting. She'd leave behind an envelope filled with cash on the kitchen counter, phone numbers and area codes written on the front. They'd phone each other every day.

Nicola spoke with her father, who lived in New York, far less often. "He's in the markets," she said, and I had the unlikely impression that he bought and sold vegetables. Before speaking with him, Nicola liked to smoke my father's British Columbian weed. I'd sit on the couch, admiring the way she bent her head back and splashed Visine drops into her eyes while still on the phone, and the way she seemed to forget about her father the second she hung up on him.

Nicola showed me where she hid the spare key to her house so I could come and go as I pleased, and she showed me where to shop and what clothes to wear. We went to parties together, and bars and clubs. The salon that cut Nicola and her mother's hair now cut mine. Nicola's friends became my friends over countless late nights at her house. Her parents might have chosen to travel and live in other cities, but I felt like I was travelling every time I left my front door.

But I was a visitor, a tourist, in Nicola's life. She kept me at arm's length, like she did everyone, always maintaining an extra distance, as if she was ready to leave her friends before they left her. I always imagined that in any one of her expensive handbags she carried her passport and enough money to buy an airline ticket to anywhere in the world.

"I want to take you to a real cool place," she told me one night. "But once you get on the plane, you can't get off. Don't fight where you're going."

She placed a paper dot of LSD on my tongue and I shivered in fear and excitement. Nothing happened at first, until Nicola took me to her bedroom and I began to feel the distinct personalities of each of her handbags, which were scattered on the floor.

"You're tripping," Nicola said. It took me a while to realize she was naked. She lay down on the bed. "Let's have sex."

"I can't," I said.

Nicola smiled, or her body smiled, or something like that, I couldn't make sense of it. "I know you're a virgin. It's okay."

"No, you don't understand. I can't see properly." Nicola's pubic hair was coloured like a rainbow, her nipples glowed.

"Don't fight the drug," she said. "Just breathe and go with it."

I breathed and went with it, and when I told Nicola what I thought was happening to her pubic hair she laughed. "It's the only rainbow you're ever going to catch."

Travelling with Nicola was a great way to live, much better than making birds in the basement. Nicola was my tour guide, able to handle anything, including my parents, people I regarded as foreigners who for some unknown reason I'd been forced to spend a regrettably extended period of time with.

"You have a really nice home, Emily," Nicola had said on her first visit, casting a critical eye on the decor. My mother thanked her, slightly taken aback by her familiar tone. Emily had always treated the girls I'd brought back to the house as if they were her friends, but she never treated them as if they were her equals. She seemed confused by Nicola, even as she tried to place her under her protective wing.

"You are a bit young to be left alone in the house, aren't you?"

Nicola, who'd taken my virginity and given me LSD all on the same night, smiled evasively.

"Did you do the renovations yourself?" she asked.

My mother said that she had, and gave her a tour of the house, which I could tell came up short in Nicola's estimation. What my mother lacked was style, the sort of style I could find over at Nicola's house, with its low-slung furniture and designer plants and perfectly fitted cabinetry. There was too much personality in our house.

It was Duncan, standing by the window, watching the fucking yuppies my mother helped bring into the neighbourhood, who seemed to have a better sense of what was going on. After Nicola had been given her tour of the house, she'd walked up to him in the living room and said, "Isn't it a shame the area is changing, Mr. Gray?" and my father had turned and stared at her without saying a word, until eventually she'd backed away.

"Have you slept with her?" he'd asked me later, when we were alone. "And don't lie because I know you've been stealing dope from my box."

I nodded. "Yeah."

"I guess you don't need any info."

"No."

"Good. I don't think she does either." Duncan looked at me with a tenderness I found abhorrent. "Just be careful," he warned, and I wasn't sure if he was talking about condoms or Nicola.

I could tell he didn't like Nicola. It was almost as if he believed she had something to do with what was happening across the street. He appeared to find the new people moving into our area more frightening than the members of the Arizona cult he'd once documented.

"They only care about money, Emily. Money, money, money. They aren't interested in film. They just want to see *blockbusters*!"

Gone, my father ranted, was the bookstore with the creaky floorboards. Gone too the shop that sold bridal gowns and nurses uniforms. "They've even renovated the hardware store," he cried. "Remember when they used to display toilet seats in the window?"

There'd been a time when Duncan had wanted to rip apart the city and uncover the creeks and ravines that he claimed had all been paved over with gridlike roads. Now it seemed that he wanted to preserve everything that he'd once professed to despise. To me, the few stores that remained untouched felt like my father's study, unpleasant, failing places of little or no value.

My mother would slip me money so I could take Nicola out to see the blockbusters my father railed against. But, despite what my father might have thought of her, Nicola wasn't really interested in seeing those movies either. Instead we went to bars and clubs where the kind of money Emily gave me didn't get me very far. Worst of all, now that Duncan knew about my drug habit, he'd taken to hiding his stash.

Actually, it wasn't my drug habit so much as it was Nicola's, who had a seemingly endless supply of money and friends. The more I kept thinking she and I were travelling to places I'd never been to before, the closer I actually came to ending up right where I'd begun, in a house full of people drinking and shouting and smoking. Some evenings I'd retreat to Nicola's bedroom, hoping she would join me. Sometimes, Nicola and her friends would go out and leave me there. I knew I was falling behind.

She was, to be an idiot about it, my rainbow, my pot of gold. Regrettably, she saw things a bit differently, especially when she'd come back home and find me in her bed, wrapped in her satin sheets. "It's only sex," she eventually told me, shoving me off the bed. "You need to go home."

"I know," I said, but I didn't. I didn't have a clue. Later, when I was back in my own house, my first course of action was to go down to the basement and roll the last of my father's weed that I'd stashed away in the furnace room, under a pile of wingless bird bodies. I propped open a window, smoked my joint, and warily eyed the birds. At some point, I'd just stopped making them, had walked away from these half-formed entities in mid-creation, much as Nicola had walked away from me.

Ever since my experience with Nicola's handbags, I'd begun to imagine the feelings of common objects, and now could feel the birds' sadness, which I resented. I didn't owe them anything; as far as I was concerned they could rot down here. "Go away," I shouted, kicking a pile of bird wings on the floor. But they had nowhere to go. I leaned down, picked up the scattered wings, and began to tie them to their bodies, bird after bird, until every last one was whole and complete.

# Made for You

A FEW DAYS LATER Philip and I went on an excursion for supplies. My presence was unnecessary, but I wanted to cruise the wide, straight, peopleless streets. There was something about the emptiness of the suburbs that I found soothing. Philip drove with a purposeful, manufactured ease; he kept his distance from other cars, never allowed the speedometer's red needle to jump above the speed limit, and gently cruised his way to full stops, looking left then right then left again before pulling away.

"Philip, dead people drive faster than you do."

Philip took a sip of iced tea, slowing down in compensation for his decreased road awareness, and made no reply. The bottle he drank from must have been twice the size of his bladder. Nothing, I reflected, seemed to come in normal sizes any more; it was all Oversized, Up-Sized, X-Large, and Tall.

At Home Depot, Philip and I bought a new zinc cutter for the wing weights and a few packages of sandpaper. There were always countless items that needed to be picked up. The job usually fell to Philip, who'd drive through the streets of Mississauga in search of ribbons and thumb tacks, paper clips, a vacuum cleaner, telephones, and, last winter, a Douglas fir Christmas tree that he'd decorated with lights, tinsel, and silver balls. I knew that he was looking forward to buying another tree this Christmas and, just to toy with him, I suggested we pick up a synthetic one at Home Depot. We could take it out each year, I said, and then stuff it back inside its box when the season was over.

These kinds of suggestions greatly upset Philip. Authenticity was important to him. The bird factory may have been located in an industrial park, directly next door to a company that imported lamps from sweatshops in mainland China, but every one of our birds came with a "Certificate of Authenticity" that guaranteed they were *Individually Hand-Crafted. Made From the Finest Materials. Designed So No Two Are Alike.*

The certificate had been Julia's idea. She'd said, "Let them think they're being built by elves," and, while Philip was no magic elf, he did take the guarantee quite seriously. The only time I'd ever thought he'd quit was when I'd suggested we start making birds out of plastic.

Philip lived in the country. He had shown me pictures of his trailer along with the property deeded to him by his grandfather shortly after he began working for me. He planned to build a proper house there one day, and, as we pulled out of Home Depot past pickup trucks piled high with building supplies, I asked him how his plans were coming along.

"The foundations are in and I've started building the frame," he said. "It'll be finished by winter."

"So soon?" His answer took me by surprise. Somehow I never thought he'd get round to it.

"Do you want to drive over and see it?"

Philip had never asked me over before and I'd never offered to visit. "Why not," I shrugged. I didn't feel like going back to work and, anyway, I was curious to see what Philip was up to.

Philip flicked on his indicator and made a left turn onto another impossibly straight road, this one with seamless, fresh black tar. It was like looking down Julia's Fallopian tubes – not an obstruction in sight. We drove through a landscape of gas stations, fast-food outlets, warehouses, pet stores – a strangely transportable, impermanent present – where everything was built to be knocked down again. Less than fifteen minutes later, the suburbs began to slip away and we entered rolling countryside where weather-beaten barns lay stranded like ships in a sea churned brown by new residential construction.

"When did you start building the house?" I asked.

"Six weeks ago. I've been getting up at five-thirty, and working at night until it's dark out."

"After a full day at the bird factory? Why haven't you said anything?" To me, Philip had appeared unaffected by the challenge, showing no outward signs of fatigue, irritability, or excitement. Either that, or I just hadn't bothered to notice his behaviour. I hoped it wasn't that.

Philip's secret hideaway was located in a small, protected valley where development, which needed flat, open fields, had not yet ventured. At the bottom of the valley lay the river and Philip's trailer.

"Home," he said, parking the car; he wasn't pointing to his trailer, but the large stacks of precut lumber rising from beside the road.

We walked around the foundation, its concrete shell dug deep into the ground, stopping when we reached the gently sloping back lawn. I heard the sound of water.

"That's the river," Philip said. "It runs past my property line." Framing the view with his hands, like a cameraman composing a shot, he said, "I'm building the house so you'll be able to see if from almost every room." We strolled to the riverbank. Philip bent down and carefully selected some flat, round stones to skip on the water.

"I've always wanted my own house. I moved around a lot when I was growing up. My father left when I was four and he never gave my mom any money, so we went wherever she could find work. It wasn't my mom's fault, but I hated moving, even if I was leaving a place I didn't like. I figured that all I'd be doing was going to another place that I'd like even less."

Philip had revealed more about himself in these last few seconds than during the year he'd worked at the bird factory. Not sure how to respond, I watched him skip several stones. They bounced across the water five or six times. He'd obviously had a lot practice.

"I think having a house is important," he continued. "For stability. Then, if I had a family, we wouldn't have to move."

"I suppose you're right," I said, thinking that even though I hadn't moved around all that much in my life, I'd never felt all that stable.

The cold was beginning to sink through the lining of my jacket. I wrapped my arms around my body and suggested we head to the car.

"I'm lonely," Philip said, without moving.

I nodded, but kept myself from looking at him. "I guess we're all lonely, in one way or another."

We decided to stop at McDonald's on our way back to the bird factory. Philip called Tamara, who was working that day, to see what she wanted. "No pickles or cheese," he said, handing back my cellphone. "Plus she wants a Diet Coke." Her special order made Philip anxious and he insisted we park the car rather than go to the drive-through so he could put in his request directly at the counter. It was the only way, he claimed, that he could make sure they were doing it right.

When we arrived back with the food, Tamara met us holding a dozen birds in her arms. They were all seagulls, with pulled-back wings and blood-red beaks. She was taking them to the weight room. I couldn't help noticing how robust, how *buxom*, she looked, as if she were about to dump her birds into a big pot and cook up something delicious.

"Did you remember to ask for no cheese?"

Her question prompted Philip to rummage noisily through the paper bags of food and pull out her hamburger, with its special red sticker affixed to the wrapper. The sticker said: Made For You.

"No pickles either," he said.

Tamara's birds, exhibiting some instinct for escape, began to slide out of her arms. I moved forward to help her. She smelled, on this bleak autumn day, of hot summer rock and suntan lotion.

"I'm always taking on more than I can handle," she laughed, dumping the birds on the table and grabbing the hamburger from Philip, who reminded her again that it came without pickles. "So," she asked, "where did you guys go? I've been the only one here for hours."

There was some anxiety in her voice. Clearly, she did not like to be left by herself. I wondered if she saw her children as good company, or if they just made her feel less alone.

"I took him to see the house," Philip said.

"How cool is *that* place."

"You've been there?" I asked, surprised.

"Sure. I've been over a few times with the kids. Don't you think he should put a cedar deck out back? It would be a great place to hang out and soak up some rays."

Philip almost never went out in the sun. He'd told me at the beginning of summer that he was allergic to it. Just a little exposure, he'd said, and his skin would break out into itchy hives that became infected if he scratched too hard. He was a man of winter.

"I was thinking more of a patio," Philip said. "But maybe a deck would be good."

"Maybe you could build both," said Tamara, happily munching on her special-order hamburger, not really caring, I felt, what Philip did or did not do at the back of his house. It suddenly occurred to me that Philip had started building his home shortly after she'd walked through the front door of the bird factory. *He* cared about what she wanted because clearly he wanted the house to be for her.

"I'm living with my parents right now," Tamara was saying. "We don't get along so well these days. They keep telling me I've screwed up my life, like they haven't screwed up theirs. It's great to get out of there and go to Philip's. He's bought the kids little hard hats and makes them glue things together. They love it." She leaned over and gave Philip an affectionate pinch on his bearded cheek.

I pushed aside the birds to clear a space on the table for my oversized drink. "I saw one of your birds the other day," I said.

"Get out! I've hardly made any. Where was it?"

*In a fertility clinic.* "In a store," I said.

"That's so cool. How can you tell it's mine?"

"I just can. I think I'm better at spotting the differences in my birds than in people."

"I totally know what you mean. It's like my kids. I can spot one of their moods a mile away."

I could only remember the name of one of her children. Carson. It was a terrible name, the kind that attached itself to cropped hair and protruding ears, so I was surprised, after Tamara plucked a photograph out of her purse, to see a child with sensitive almond-shaped eyes, coffee-coloured skin, and straight, long, honest hair – the kind only five-year-olds seem to possess.

Looking at the photo it struck me as odd that Julia and I had never sat down to discuss, as couples do – or were supposed to do – the potential names we wished to attach to our off-spring. *Jack, John, Jill, Jane.*

Tamara slipped another photo into my hand and I passed the first one to Philip, who vigilantly wiped his hands on a paper napkin before accepting it.

"That's Oliver," she said.

Like most childless men, the photos of other people's children held very little interest for me. I looked down at the picture, but only because it was expected of me. "They look like great kids," I said, only half-insincerely, handing the second photo over to Philip. He refused to put the first one down and held both of them up for scrutiny.

"They *are* great kids," Tamara said. "But I should have waited. Everything just got away from me, like their father. But you know how Caribbean men are."

"Not really."

"Your loss," she said, grinning.

"Where is he now?" I asked.

"Dominica," Philip answered, handing back the photos. Clearly, Tamara had discussed this with him before.

"Is that where you met?" I asked her. "In Dominica?"

"No, I'd never even heard of it before. We met at a bar in Toronto. He said he was up here on business." She laughed, as if the thought of the father of her children being engaged in anything so productive was funny. "A couple of months later he asked me to go back down with him. I think his visa had run out.

"Then, two weeks after I got there I found out I was pregnant with Carson. I don't know how it happened. I've always been careful. Sometimes, they just slip through." Tamara smiled as if the thought pleased her. "I thought of having an abortion, but Dee said children were a gift from God and abortion was a sin. Of course my parents absolutely freaked. I was only eighteen."

Just as I was beginning to wonder if God had anything to do with my problems, Hans strolled into the bird factory. He was splattered in paint and wore a bandanna around his head, to keep his hair clean. Hans only worked eight to ten hours a week, but lately he seemed to always be in the factory. He'd slip in from his own studio at the precise point he found himself the most bored and irritated, and would take out his frustration on me, or Philip, or the world in general.

Hans rolled his eyes. "How I hate this place. I am going mad. It's not enough that I have to make these birds, they've built a nest inside my head. They won't leave me alone. I dream about them! I cannot escape. I want a raise."

I laughed.

"I know you pay Lurch more than me. I've been here almost a year. I deserve it."

"Philip gets more because he works full-time. He does more and he's been here longer. What I pay you is fair."

"Fair? You have the morality of an American Express card."

"Hans, this is my company."

"Company? You make wooden birds."

"So do you, Hans. Or is your presence here an illusion?"

Hans regarded me as his tormentor, but I was as much a victim of the birds as he, more so because they'd followed me all the way to the fertility clinic, where one dangled above all the hopefuls.

"Life is an illusion," said Hans hopelessly. "In the end, we are all just making birds."

"Then you should be happy," I said. "Because that's exactly what you're doing."

"Will the two of you *please* shut up," Tamara interrupted, pulling out three cigarettes, one for each of us.

I accepted her offer of a cigarette, tucking it into my breast pocket for later use, and thinking that, for all our quarrelling, or maybe because of it, I felt closer to Hans than anyone else in the bird factory. He was ruled by a mysterious misery I found particularly calming. Meanwhile Philip, ever quiet except for his one emotional outburst by the river, had a goodness to him that I could barely fathom. I thought of the way he'd held Tamara's photos, looking at them with curious, almost personal interest and remembered how I'd mocked his request for production manager business cards. I now realized that all he'd wanted was an official title to take with him to the bank, so he could get a loan to help build his house. Why couldn't I have just printed him the cards?

Tamara, accepting a light from Hans, started up again with her life history. It was confusing – she had one kid, then another; she lived with Dee's family, seven to a house; she moved out, she moved back in; they fought and made up and fought again. She said something about the windsurfers, with their parrots on the sails. But in the end, it didn't work out and she'd come home four years and two kids later.

"That's okay," she said as if to answer our concern for her. "I believe everything happens for a reason."

"You think there's a reason for all this?" Hans said with a sweeping arc of his hand. "Are we being punished?"

I started to clear up the room, to show that lunch was over. Rising out of a narrow copper vase on the floor close to where Tamara was sitting was a large peacock feather, a gift from Julia, who'd given it to me when I'd first moved out to Mississauga. Under my neglectful care, the shimmering blue eyes were covered with cataracts of dust. I leaned over and gently blew the dust away.

"You shouldn't have one of those indoors," Tamara said.

"Why not?" I asked. "My wife gave it to me."

"Didn't you know that peacock feathers are unlucky? They have the Evil Eye."

"Well that explains it," said Hans. "We've been living under the bad spell of a bird."

# A Crack in the Wall

THERE WAS SOMETHING disruptive about the name Chantal, something suggestive and improper. What was needed at this moment was an Edna, an Edith, a name without promise.

The lusciously named Chantal was wearing a nurse's outfit. The effect was more theatrical than professional – the fertility clinic was not a hospital – and she greeted us with the slightly distracted, inward-looking eyes of an actor just before a performance. She was blonde and petite and stood beside an imposing television set perched on a wheeled metal rack, the kind I'd last seen in high school. Taped to the blank screen was a piece of paper. It said, "In Vitro Fertilization. Is It Right For You?"

Julia and I took our seats in the second from last row. Almost all the chairs were occupied.

Unlike the general waiting room, there were no distracting magazines. The men, empty-handed, sat at rigid attention beside their spouses, staring not at Chantal, who warranted it, but at the blank television set as if hoping the lights would go down and they could settle into anonymity. The women looked more determined, brusquer, as if they were waiting at a transit stop and the bus was late.

Only one couple seemed to fully acknowledge each other. They sat in their chairs, gripping each other's hands with a fervent and desperate passion, defiant smiles on their faces. *They would get through this together.*

It made me want to hit them.

"Let's start with the basics," said Chantal once she was satisfied that we, her patients, had all taken our seats. "In vitro fertilization, what is it?" Chantal took a confident step toward her audience. "Basically, it's the process whereby we extract a woman's eggs and fertilize them outside of the body, in a laboratory, with her partner's sperm. After two to six days, we reinsert the fertilized embryos – eggs whose cells have successfully divided – back into the woman's uterus. This is called an embryo transfer. The hope is that the embryo will grow and lead to a successful pregnancy. If it doesn't take the first time, the process can be repeated."

Chantal smiled.

*We shouldn't be here*, I thought – it was as if we were in some sort of graduate class where, unlike other graduate classes, everyone had to fail the previous course in order to get here.

This was not a moment, or a subject, to share with strangers. It wasn't fair. It wasn't appropriate. It wasn't *dignified*. We should have had our own private meeting, if not with Dr. Henderson, who was obviously too busy with golf and conferences, then at least with some frumpy old shrew who, unlike Chantal, didn't radiate sexual vitality while saying, "The female's egg is retrieved from the ovary by placing a needle through the vaginal wall."

Blithely unaware of my animosity, Chantal continued with her speech. "An important procedure which complements in vitro is called ICSI, otherwise know as intracytoplasmic sperm injection. Rather than let sperm fertilize the egg itself, we select, grade, and inject individual sperm directly into the egg."

I looked at Julia from the corner of my eye. She sat with smart attention, her back straight, arms folded over her lap, head bent slightly forward in riveted attention. Julia had been taught the essential rudiments of good public behaviour. She looked like an earnest, well-behaved student and, as punishment, I turned to stare at her and planned to keep staring until she noticed me. Fortunately, Chantal turned off the lights before I had a chance to feel foolish.

Chantal purred, "And now I'm going to play a video." For just one brief moment, before the tape started to roll, it was dark and peaceful and reminded me of the days when I'd join my mother in the basement watching Duncan's film.

Why hadn't I phoned him? He was probably sitting behind his bankruptcy-auctioned desk pretending, as I was, though with far greater forces of concentration, that everything that was happening wasn't happening. If he just sat it out things would take care of themselves, go away, vanish. I told myself that I hadn't revealed my father's illicit affair to Julia because I feared she'd tell my mother, but I wasn't entirely convinced that was the reason. Duncan had impregnated someone. *That* was it. For Julia – for both of us – that would have been, however much we might have wished otherwise, the centre of the story, the meaning of it: he'd succeeded where we had so far failed. Neither I nor Duncan had called each other because to do so we would have to acknowledge different, though equally unpleasant, facts.

The twenty-minute video presented the tribulations of a couple who, like all of us sitting in this room, were attempting to conceive a child. We watched the couple sit for their first appointment with their fertility doctor, who was wearing a white overcoat like Chantal; listened as they listened to the procedures that would be administered to them and so, therefore, to us. The video couple nodded with frank, amiable faces, shades of concern around their eyes – they looked as if they were selecting a washing machine.

When the film ended and the lights came back on, we fidgeted in our chairs. Chantal said, "Any questions?" Nobody had any. Shortly afterwards, we gathered up our belongings and filed out of the room.

Back at the house, Julia made a fire. Her past experience never counted for much with fires; she was careless and impatient, and just threw the wood over crumpled newspaper, smothering the flames. Julia knew how to make a proper fire – she'd once shown me a picture of herself as a Girl Scout and made a joke of the merit badges that ran down the length of her shirt sleeve, including one for fire-making. Yet here in the house she steadfastly refused to arrange the logs in a teepee, with kindling and newspaper placed in the hollow centre, as one was supposed to do, as she'd been taught to do. It drove me crazy.

"I don't like the idea of Dr. Henderson selecting my sperm," I said, staring at the crack in the wall. It was definitely growing.

"I guess that's his job."

"I guess so," I said.

In my pocket was a cost sheet, which the lovely Chantal had handed out like flyers to a strip club when the seminar was over. While Julia attended to her fire, I examined the price of Dr. Henderson's expertise.

**Standard IVF package pricing: $7,800 with all monitoring included**
**(Cash discounted price)**

Included Services:

- Ovarian stimulation monitoring
- Anaesthesia for egg (ova) retrieval
- Ovum retrieval
- Fertilization and culture of ova
- Embryo transfer

Excluded Services:

|  |  |
|---|---|
| • Prescreening tests | $500.00 |
| • Medications | $3,500.00 |
| • ICSI – intracytoplasmic sperm injection | $1,000.00 |
| • Storage of frozen sperm or embryos one year | $750.00 |
| • Storage fee for each additional year | $300.00 |
| • Hospitalization/complications | N/A |

**If your cycle is cancelled there is a non-refundable fee of $500.00**

**Embryo and sperm freezing are optional**

I turned on the television to calm myself. *The Amazing Race* was on. Various competing couples – husbands and wives, bowling moms, even a dwarf – were rushing around the world trying to win a million dollars. The teams were in Uruguay. The country looked terrible, cloudy and cool, and, at least along the coast, half-built, a place I'd never want to visit. I had nothing against Uruguayans and obviously they'd wanted to show the best of themselves, so I was mildly distressed for them about the state of their country. "I wouldn't want to go there," I said to Julia, but she wasn't listening. It wouldn't be long, I reflected, before they'd make a show about infertility, where distressed couples would face difficult tasks devised by Dr. Henderson. The first person to get a picture of their newborn on his desk would win a million dollars and a university scholarship for their child.

I glanced down at the sheet again. Each attempt at IVF was going to cost us well over ten thousand dollars. It was the sort of reality I didn't care for. How many birds would I need to sell to afford this? Hundreds? Thousands?

An entire flock.

I crumpled the paper in my hand. "Here," I said, "more fuel for the fire." Julia, not knowing what it was, threw it in the grate and I watched it burn into nothingness.

# Just When You Think

"JUST TELL ME YOU HAVEN'T BEEN SMOKING."

"I haven't been smoking."

Julia disdainfully held a dirty work shirt of mine and fished from its pocket a cigarette, crinkled and limp from a day or two outside its protective box. Her family was coming over for a visit and she'd been cleaning the house.

"Is this yours?"

"No."

"Then whose is it?"

"It's Tamara's," I said, remembering how I'd slipped it into my pocket for later use. I'd been sloppy.

"Who's Tamara?"

"Someone I hired to work at the factory. Haven't I told you about her? Why are you going through my pockets, anyway?"

"Why are you having cigarettes with strange women?"

"Tamara's not a strange woman, she's an *employee*. She was probably about to light up, realized that she had to hang up a bird or something, and handed me the cigarette for safe-keeping. I put it in my pocket and we both forgot about it." This sounded weak even to my ears.

Julia held the offending item between the tips of her fingers as if they were Tamara's underwear.

"I have to take all these drugs, I'm being poked and prodded and injected every single day. We're about to spend tens of thousands of dollars – and all you had to do was stop smoking."

"And I have!"

"Then what's this?"

"An unsmoked cigarette. If I *was* smoking, there wouldn't be an entire cigarette in my shirt pocket. I'd have already smoked it."

"Does that mean that anyone walking around with a full pack of cigarettes is a non-smoker?"

"It's possible."

"Luke, I don't care what you do to yourself. If you want to rot your lungs out, rot your lungs out. But things are getting serious and you're acting like a child. I'm not going to keep watch over you. I'm not your mother."

"That's why I married you," I said and began to take off my clothes.

"What are you doing? My parents will be here any minute."

"Getting serious. They don't have to give us seminars for this."

I took hold of Julia and pushed her down on the bed, pinning her beneath my body. Who needed the fertility clinic? We could do it on our own. I'd heard it said a good marksman directs the arrow with his mind. Perhaps my failure had been one of imagination. Perhaps if I concentrated. Sometimes, when positions were reversed and Julia lay on top of me, she'd lean forward and let her hair drop down. It was as if I'd poked my head through a silk curtain. It was beautiful in there, secretive and protective – but secretive and protective didn't get you babies.

Julia tucked her hands under my shoulders and pushed. "Get off."

"I'm trying to make you pregnant."

"Not like this you aren't. You think you're just going to stick it in?"

"You want romance?" I asked incredulously.

"I don't want what you're doing."

I rolled off.

The ceiling, white and bare and flat, reminded me of Julia's belly. I closed my eyes and the image, slowly forming, of Rosemary, heavy with my father's child, came into my head.

Julia lifted herself off the bed. Without her weight on the mattress, I felt my body rise. "I have to get ready," she said.

Julia walked down the hall to the washroom and I heard the metallic ping as she locked the door. I opened my eyes and looked at my watch, fighting a desperate urge not to fetch the cigarette and go for a smoke.

I greeted the Riddells with a big, dishonest smile. There they were: Maureen, Lloyd, and Barry.

"Where's my sister?"

I pointed upstairs.

"What's she doing?"

"Drink?" I asked, ignoring Barry and leading Lloyd and Maureen into the living room. They should have felt right at home – most of the furnishings came from their house. Lloyd Riddell chose the high wingback chair that sat to one side of the fireplace. It had been his favourite chair in his own home before his wife had deemed it expendable. "Scotch?" I suggested. Lloyd nodded. It was always Scotch. We kept a bottle of Glenfiddich just for him. With his fleshy face that sagged like a day-old balloon, there was a bit of the ox in him, and for fun I silently marked off his body like a butcher's chart.

"When is she coming down?" Barry demanded.

He stood at the foot of the stairs, anxious for his sister's arrival.

"I know what you want, Barry. A half and half with lots of ice."

Barry placed his hand on the banister and glowered.

"What do you say?" admonished Maureen.

Barry protested, rather violently, that he didn't want any Coke, but since that wasn't true – he always wanted a Coke – and since he'd inevitably be required to say things like "please" and "thank you," he glumly accepted my offer.

In the kitchen I poured out the drinks, including Barry's regular half-Coke, half-Diet Coke, the latter poured first or he'd complain. I made his drink in a brass-handled beer stein purchased specially for him.

It was hard for bloated Barry to sneak up on people – he was too loaded down with sugar and snacks – but he managed to slip into the kitchen undetected. "I don't like you," he said.

I handed Barry his beer stein. "That's okay. I don't like me either."

Was Down syndrome transmittable? Did it snake its way up the family tree, ready to inject its genetic poison? Or was it random, without malice, like accidentally stepping on a bee?

"You're an *ass*hole."

"That's a big, bad ugly word, Barry. Why don't you go out to the living room and say that in front of your parents."

"*Ass*hole," he repeated.

"Bigger asshole," I answered.

Barry took a greedy gulp of his half-Coke, half-Diet Coke concoction and wiped his mouth with the back of his hand. He began to talk to me about a baseball game, about extension cords, about anything that came into his mind: *Have you ever driven a Jaguar? You should mow your lawn. I bet you don't know what a Datsun is. My sister is unhappy.*

"What was that you just said about your sister?" The drinks were in my hand; Lloyd's Scotch, white wine with one ice cube for Maureen.

"She's sad. She doesn't like you."

Julia was still upstairs, in the bathroom; things weren't exactly chipper and wonderful between us, but how would Barry know?

"Has anyone said anything to you?" I asked. Barry shook his head. "Then why would you say something like that?"

"She's my sister," he answered, before losing interest and walking back into the living room.

Maureen Riddell took her glass and sipped her wine with far more grace but no less greed than her son. I walked over and placed Lloyd's Scotch in his hand. Julia thought her father drank too much – the reddened, irritated skin around his neck pointed to a potential problem – but never before had I seen him siphon off a glass in one angry gulp. It may be, I thought, that he and Maureen had detected Julia's unhappiness as well.

"Barry," he commanded, "go up and get your sister."

Lloyd's words galvanized his son; he rushed for upstairs, only momentarily halted by Maureen's command to put down his stein of Coke on the coffee table. As he galloped away, I noticed how Lloyd watched him with a mixture of pride and concern.

"He's got a girlfriend," Lloyd said.

"Really, who?" I asked, trying to sound interested, relieved that I wouldn't be talking about their daughter.

Maureen answered, "Her name is Christy. He met her at his residence. She lives two floors above him. They get along very well. She's had dinner with us several times."

"She's not a girl, she's a woman," corrected Lloyd. This fact evidently disturbed him a great deal and I fetched the bottle of Scotch from the kitchen and poured him another drink. "She's older than he is," he added ominously.

"Is that a problem?" I asked.

"She's thirty-two."

Maureen rooted for an explanation. "We're worried about what they might be doing. If they're aware of the . . . consequences."

"Of course they're not aware of the consequences!" thundered Lloyd. "They're all retarded!"

He wasn't referring solely to his son and Christy and the other special-needs occupants at the residential community, but also to the staff who worked there. "The director of the building tells me he's monitoring the situation. I asked him if that means he knows what's going on when my son is alone in her apartment, or she's alone in his."

"The apartments are professionally staffed, with lots of supervision," soothed Maureen.

"Do they supervise in the middle of the night?"

A burst of laughter from upstairs distracted his anger and I noticed how he swung his head indulgently toward the sounds of his children. His two childless children. With one, he evidently worried. And with the other, did he not sometimes wonder? Why hadn't his daughter become a mother? What prevented her? They'd been careful never to ask. Maureen had mentioned, once or twice, and in passing, that the furniture we'd inherited from her was unsuitable for young children, but that was the extent of it. Julia must have had something to do with this, a way of keeping a distance from her parents.

"I want you to talk to him," said Lloyd.

"Talk to who?"

"Barry. I'm his father. He won't listen to me." I wondered if this was true, seeing the way Barry had just rushed up the stairs, but I got his point. "I want him to work for you at the factory for a while. I'll pay his wages, but I don't want him to know."

I paused. "I'm not sure I understand what working for me will accomplish." I had no need of Barry at the factory; I had no need of Tamara for that matter, but there she was, eating pickle-free hamburgers and telling stories about drowning windsurfers.

"Get into his confidence, find out what's going on, and report back to me."

"You want me to *spy* on him?"

Maybe I should have taken their request as a compliment, proof of acceptance into the family, but all I could think was that the Riddells wanted me to do their dirty work for them.

"I don't want him getting tangled up with some hussy. He's only twenty-six." Julia's footsteps could be heard above and Lloyd leaned forward in his chair to gesture privacy. "And I don't want you to tell Julia."

I looked over to Maureen, in amazement. She nodded her approval. "It would just complicate things," she said.

Complications, it seemed, were something the Riddells did their best to steer clear of. As Julia came down the stairs, looking refreshed and relaxed, Barry in tow, I was amazed and just a little frightened by her steady composure, which hid so much and hid it so well. Her parents would know nothing of what had happened upstairs, I thought. Could I deceive Julia as well as she deceived her family? I thought of my mother and the secrets I already kept from her and from Julia.

"I'm sorry," she said, leaning over and kissing her father's cheek, distracting his attention away from the glass she removed from his hand. "I was just taking a bath."

To her mother, she smiled; with Barry she snuck a hand under his shirt and kneaded his back with the tips of her fingers, a physical reminder of past years when he'd suffered from congestion and she'd prop him up and rub his back until his eyes closed and he no longer felt as if he were drowning. But she wouldn't look at me.

"I've just been talking to Luke," Lloyd said to his son. "He told me that he needs help at his company and asked me if you could work for him."

Barry, impressed by his father's seriousness and pleased by the attention, nodded. And my wife, for the first time since coming down the stairs, appeared tenderly disposed toward me. Obviously, Julia believed I'd asked her brother to come work for me as penance for my behaviour.

And I did nothing to dissuade her. It was disgraceful to take credit, but take credit I did.

I noticed Barry didn't thank me for the job but instead kept close to his sister, who continued to rub his back. The only one in the room incapable of deception, he must have sensed something was wrong.

Now that it was Julia who was suffering, there was the very real question of who would rub *her* back. I suppose that duty rested upon me, her husband, but the tips of my fingers felt bruised.

"So what do you say?" Julia said to Barry, gently prodding him toward me.

Barry looked cornered.

"Thank you," he mumbled, and shook my hand.

# Pins and Needles

IT WAS RAINING when I pulled up to Barry's special-needs residence, a light, windless drizzle that showed no signs of letting up. Barry stood outside the front door, beneath a protective, concrete overhang. Despite the faint warmth of the fall day, his body was swaddled in a heavy brown parka with a fur-lined hood that swallowed up most of his head. He was not alone. A woman, also wrapped inside a matching brown parka – it must have been Christy – stood beside him, a pink hand enfolded into his.

The coats weren't the only articles of clothing out of season. Christy wore a wide-brimmed summer hat, pinned to her head at an angle she must have thought skilfully fashionable but that looked instead as if it had been in a losing battle with her parka hood.

Christy was the reason I was here – she was the older, experienced woman that Lloyd Riddell felt threatened his son's innocence and stability. As I stepped out of the car to introduce myself, I noticed the dress shoes and the flowery summer dress she wore beneath her unzipped parka.

Barry, with aching formality, said, "This is my brother-in-law, Luke Gray."

I extended my hand.

"Nice to meet you."

She was definitely older than Barry, but it was hard to tell from looking at her by how much.

"I am Christy Gadd," she said, giggling. It was a woman's giggle, full of knowingness and good humour.

She walked us to the car and stood on the curb as we sped away. I watched her in the rear-view mirror, her image becoming smaller and smaller. Then I turned the corner and she slipped out of sight.

"So," I said, "she's got great tits."

This was the wrong thing to say and I knew it immediately. I'd meant to be chummy and jocular. I sounded vulgar.

Barry turned away from me.

"Here," I said, reaching for a bag in the back seat. "Julia made you lunch."

I placed the bag on Barry's lap, the warmth from the food lingering on my fingers, though it was wholly imaginary because Julia had made cold sandwiches – tuna fish, with a dollop of mayo, a squeeze of lemon, some cut celery, spread between two slices of Wonderbread, a concession to Barry. I'd told Julia that I'd take Barry to McDonald's for his first day, but she'd insisted he start work on a proper nutritional footing. I watched her prepare his food thinking how bright and warm the kitchen felt. Something of that warmth had transferred itself to the bag.

I drove on for a bit, feeling anxious and invaded by Barry's company, and angry at the Riddells in general for fostering him upon me. Barry held on to Julia's lunch as if I were going to snatch it from him. He didn't say a word, just stared out the window.

"Christy seems like a real nice girl," I said.

Barry, despite himself, smiled in agreement.

"So, you have found a new victim, have you?"

Hans seemed to jump out from the shadows the moment we arrived at the factory, startling me.

"Why are you lurking by the door, Hans?" I said to him irritably. "That's just weird. This is my brother-in-law, Barry Riddell. He's going to help us out here at the factory."

"Glad to meet you, Mr. Barry Riddell." Hans clicked his heels and bowed slightly. "I am sorry we have to meet under these circumstances." He threw me a nasty look. "How could you bring another person to be tortured by these birds?"

"Speaking of birds, Hans . . ." I told Barry to grab a bird and when he did I turned off all the lights.

"Hold it up higher," I said.

There, held above his shoulders, was Hans's signature, bright and angry, written on the bird's belly in glow-in-the-dark paint, followed by "Help me! I'm dying!"

"You can't sign the birds, Hans."

"At least I have a signature," he snorted. "An identity. A point of reference. You leave no mark because you have nothing to sign."

"Those are my birds you're defacing," I answered.

"I make them, I sign them."

The lights came suddenly back on.

"Even my kids don't fight in the dark." Tamara stood with her hand on the light switch. The fluorescent intrusion caused Hans and I to blink and squint.

Barry, confused by what had just happened, still held the bird up in the air. Tamara took it out of his hands and introduced herself, then pulled up a chair and suggested he sit down beside a pile of bird wings. She sat down beside him and began to teach him how to attach the wings to the painted bodies.

I had never really thought of Tamara as a parent before. The facts of Tamara's motherhood were obvious and undeniable, of course – I'd seen the photos of Carson and Oliver, knew of their birth and existence – but from the moment she'd walked into the bird factory, I'd never been able to picture her actually *with* children, washing them, telling them stories, taking them to school, examining their ears for wax, all the mundane, confident activities parents were acknowledged to do.

Now, however, as I watched her teach Barry with that special parental ability to impart information without stooping to condescension, I found her patience deeply touching. It was clear that Barry adored her.

Over the course of the morning Tamara devised games out of making birds – five strung birds equalled five gulps of Coke – and to ward off any encroaching boredom she and Barry would attach the wrong body parts – seagull wings to flying fish bodies, for instance – and invent new names for their creations: *fish-gull*, *fird*, *seagle*.

Hans was not placated. "Why does the world always disappoint me?" he asked, angrily rubbing his eyes in frustration.

"Maybe it's the other way around."

Hans surprised me by pausing to consider the proposition.

To punish Hans for the signatures, I sent Barry to help him dip wings in the paint room. It was, as it turned out, no punishment at all. When I tiptoed over to the room and peeked in, I saw that both of them were wearing their safety masks. Barry mumbled something beneath his mask that made Hans laugh; they were like two naughty children who'd been given detention. Maybe the warmth of Julia's lunch had migrated to the factory.

We developed a routine. I drove Barry to work, I drove him home, and every day Christy was there, standing just outside the building waiting for him. He always tried to remain stoic in my presence, hanging back for just an extra second or two, before rushing out of the car to reach Christy's hands and lips. With their oversized, disjointed heads, and bodies made fat by an excess of prescription drugs and super-sized Slurpees, they were the very embodiment of love.

I'd tried to ask Barry a few leading questions and had got nowhere. I concluded I wasn't going to learn anything about Christy, and that was okay, I didn't want to. As far as I was concerned, it wasn't any of my business what the two of them got up to behind closed doors, though I suspected it was more than Lloyd Riddell could properly endorse. A part of him was no doubt proud his son was no longer a virgin, but he must have wondered, too, if Barry could be trusted to apply the necessary protection with daily, dutiful proficiency.

The irony did not escape me the morning we had to make a stop to pick up Julia's fertility drugs.

The drugs in question were at a pharmacy in Mississauga, close to the bird factory, where, according to Dr. Henderson, they were cheaper than downtown. It was a small store, unpleasantly intimate. Family-run. I left Barry in the car, telling him he could take his seat belt off, but he kept it strapped across his body, as if at any moment he might suddenly be hurled forward.

"I've come to pick up a package for Mrs. Gray," I said to the pharmacist. I was embarrassed, which I knew was stupid, and was reminded how my mother made me pick up boxes of Tampax for her. Even though my present bill came to well over fifteen hundred dollars – not an amount a teenager would normally pay – I still felt stupid and wondered how the pharmacist, who wore a white labcoat, and the woman next to him, who did not and whom I took to be his wife, had managed to corner the city market on fertility drugs. What were they up to? Had they themselves suffered from similar problems? Maybe they wanted to help others. Maybe they were just trying to make a buck. It was hard to tell.

The take-home drugs were part of the IVF treatment, the new fertility procedure we'd decided to try. It hadn't been much of a decision – in Julia's eyes there was no other option than to go on. Before, Julia had received her injections at the fertility clinic, but now she was going to self-administer two drugs from the comfort of our home – Luperon for the first ten days, and Puregon for another two weeks or so. When Chantal had said that husbands could administer the injections, all the husbands had laughed because she made it sound as if it was a way of getting back at our wives, a joke she must have used at every seminar.

Barry was still strapped into his seat belt when I returned with the drugs. He'd farted and the car smelled.

"Look," I said, holding up my bag. "Now I have lunch too."

I dropped Barry off at the factory and ran in to do a few things before leaving again. I had to return home and put the drugs in the refrigerator.

"Could you take charge of Barry?" I asked Tamara, who I'd suggested come in more often now that Barry was around.

She gave me an intimate, encouraging nod as if she knew I was unhappy taking care of Barry. And because I felt that knowing what makes someone unhappy is just as intimate as knowing what makes them joyful, there was something conspiratorial in the nod I offered back to her. Something illicit and remarkably pleasurable.

Julia was cutting tomatoes in the kitchen when I arrived home, quarter sections that fell away and rocked on their behinds like a seesaw. I reached out for one and Julia tapped me on the hand with the flat of her knife. "That's not for you," she said.

"What are you doing here?" I asked.

"Mia sounded upset over the phone. She took the day off to spend time with Tyler. I thought it would be a good idea if they came over for lunch. Here," she said, handing me a ripe quarter slice. "Take this." I took the tomato and put it in my mouth, feeling as if Julia was waiting for some sort of comment, like she'd grown the tomato herself and wanted me to report on its taste.

"I love you," I said.

"You could tell me once in a while."

"I'm telling you now."

The sight of food prepared and denied filled me with uncharitable thoughts toward Mia and her child. Did she really need to bring Tyler here, to crawl all over Julia?

I retired upstairs minutes after they arrived. Mia had come for something and it wasn't the salad. The two of them, aware of my presence, spoke in low voices that instantly provoked my interest. Tyler was less complicit, letting out the occasional squeal, which failed to interrupt his mother's conversation but filled me with a loathing of Mia. Her child felt like an accusation.

It must be that way for everyone who attended the fertility clinic. We were nothing but vacant bodies at the mercy of other people's children.

I began to feel there was a touch of triumphalism in every parent. Even if Mia had left her child at home I'd have thought she'd done so to spare Julia's feelings and not liked her for that either.

A muffled, female sob filled me with alarm. I crept over to the doorway. To my relief it was Mia.

"I don't know what to do," she snivelled.

"You don't have to do anything right now."

"He's just so depressed. He says he feels useless. We never have sex any more."

"It happens. He'll get back on his feet."

"I want him back on me," Mia said, which was funny, even clever, especially for Mia, but she didn't laugh or giggle or seem to recognize her own joke. "I think if he got out of the house a bit, saw some friends. He just spends all day inside and then, when I get home, he takes long walks. Sometimes he doesn't get back until I'm asleep. Or when I pretend to be asleep."

Then Julia made a horrible suggestion. "Maybe Luke could meet him for lunch. That would get him out of the house."

What *was* it with the Riddells? Always offering out my services, like I was a charity.

Julia called for me. There was nothing I could do but come downstairs and wait for the request.

"Mia and I were just talking about how we don't get together like we used to," Julia said with feigned casualness. "How long has it been since you and Roger have seen each other? Maybe he could pop by the bird factory one of these days for lunch."

Both women stared at me. *What a terrible thing to do to Roger*, I thought, to bring him down like this. I didn't want to know Roger was depressed because he wouldn't have wanted me to know. I hated to think what Julia might have confided to Mia.

"Sure," I said, "I'll meet him for lunch," thinking it was best to keep them happy, especially Julia, who knew that our sex life over these past few months hadn't been much better than Mia and Roger's. I simply wasn't interested, and I don't think Julia was either.

"I was just in the neighbourhood," Roger said when he met me at the bird factory for lunch the following week, though my neighbourhood wasn't the sort of place one ventured into without a purpose.

This time Tyler was his father's accessory, strapped into a front-mounted body harness. Tyler's legs, like two fat worms, wiggled in the air. The two of them, father and son, were flushed from the heat of their outdoor clothes.

"Can I help you unstrap?" I asked.

"No, that's fine, no worries."

He stood there without seeming to know what else to say.

Because it was Tuesday, and just past eleven in the morning, I didn't bother asking how Roger was doing. It was obvious how he was doing because he wasn't doing anything except walking around the bird factory with a baby strapped to his chest.

Philip was busy sanding. He raised a sawdust-covered arm in greeting. Tamara and Barry were, as usual, tying bird wings; Tamara smiled, Barry scowled. Over the past few weeks he'd become possessive about Tamara and the bird factory. He didn't like strangers.

"I hope I'm not interfering," Roger said.

*Poor bastard.* He'd lost all confidence. It was a terrible thing to know more about a person than you should. There needed to be a distance, an impenetrable barrier between men, but our wives had breached that space and exposed us to each other's problems. I was repelled by his unhappiness and lack of confidence as if it were contagious. At least in the privacy of his own smoking room, Roger could plunge himself into a wingback chair and make the world disappear; but out here his failures were obvious and real, and served only to remind me that we were not unalike, though of course he had a baby that fidgeted only a few feet away from his beating heart, while Julia and I had nothing, the sort of nothing that comes when you're trying to have something.

"Where do you want to eat?"

I listed off a number of "fine dining" restaurants conveniently located on the corners of major intersections, but Roger appeared more interested in my computer. It was from there, seated at the computer, that I cast surreptitious glances at Tamara; I liked the tightness of her back when she leaned into her work. Barry sometimes caught me looking and made a face.

"This thing doesn't even have a CD-ROM. It's a dinosaur!"

"I don't really use it," I said, not caring about my nonexistent computer system.

"You need to upgrade. You're probably running on sixteen meg of RAM, which is laughable." To show me that it was, Roger laughed. "You need to install a new hard drive, get a CD burner to back up your data." Roger unbuckled his son and placed him on the floor. It wasn't particularly clean or safe down there. "You should really design a Web site. Customers will be able to order birds on-line. We'll take pictures of your birds and put them on the Web. It wouldn't cost much. Just think, your birds will go places they've never been before." Roger was highly excited. Philip had stopped working and was nodding seriously, even Tamara seemed interested.

"They're migrating," she said, taking Barry's hand and flapping it in the air.

"A giant electronic migration," said Roger.

The birds weren't the only things migrating that fall. Roger started coming to the bird factory every day. So did Tyler. There was Barry, who I picked up outside his building each morning. And Tamara to help me watch over him. Barry had begun to ask if we could take Christy with us too.

There was obviously no thought given to whisking little Tyler into daycare. Instead, Tamara devised a playpen for him, the perimeter secured with boxes that Barry constructed and deconstructed each day. It was where Tyler slumbered on the blanketed floor, then screamed for food. From inside a blue nylon satchel Roger carried with him to work came pre-dampened wipes, toys, talcum powder, and diapers.

Roger would pull out a milk bottle, wriggle the nipple into his child's mouth, and wait absent-mindedly until his satiated child began to push the bottle away with flailing hands.

Hans surveyed my crowded domain.

"Look at us," he said to me, "a room of failures."

He was right, of course.

"No one buys my paintings. I work here, making birds, that is what they buy." Hans said. "And your unemployed friend with the baby. He works here too. And the single mother who humped a beach vendor. And there is Lurch. Do you see the way he looks at her? Or how he tries not to look at her? Lurch is in love."

"Yes," I admitted.

"He is building a nest for Tamara. I don't think she knows it. Or maybe she does. I think Lurch will make a good father for her children. He is steady. A great bore. That's what the Lurches of the world are like, you know. Ripe for the plucking."

There'd been a time – not too long ago, I had to remind myself – when it was just Philip and me, quietly making birds, the morning sun crawling up over our east-fronted windows, the radio pleasantly announcing the disasters of the day. In winter, when the two of us would lock up and head for home, we'd walk out to our cars and watch our headlights burn through the cold darkness knowing that we'd see each other the following day. Then Hans arrived. Then Tamara, then Barry. And now Roger and his infant son. Every corner of the factory was occupied.

"And what about the employer of this bird place? Who is he? He's unhappy, like the rest of us here. You are married and still I see you looking at Tamara."

"There's no harm in looking, Hans."

But there *was* harm. There was harm in the fact that I no longer felt like making love to my wife, harm that I was selfish and petty for thinking the fertility drugs had stolen the beauty from her face. The drugs exhausted Julia, puffed her out and made her skin look like grainy off-white paper – punch three rings in her body, slip her into a binder, close the cover, and let her sleep.

At this stage of the treatment, Julia had to go to the clinic every day and have her ovaries and hormone levels checked. Then later she'd phone the clinic for the result and adjust her Luperon dosage accordingly. The first time we'd tried it at home, Julia had handed me the needle, slipped off her pants, and sat down on the edge of the bed. "You do it," she'd said, and I'd pulled off the plastic stopper and felt immediately faint at the sight of the glinting needle, irrationally fearful I'd accidentally puncture myself. There was a hope, encouraged by the fertility clinic, that administering your wife's injections was a bonding experience. It wasn't. Julia disinfected a small patch of skin on her right upper thigh while I sucked up the Luperon with the needle and flicked the syringe to get out the air bubbles. Then I'd pinched the patch of disinfected skin with two sweaty fingers. The rising mound of flesh glistened. I'd never had a problem with needles before, but at that moment I felt peculiarly nauseous. To my discredit, I'd turned away just before plunging the needle in. From then on, Julia injected herself behind closed doors.

Barry, who let out an excited yelp over lunch, disturbed my recollections. Lunchtime was always a happy moment for him. I watched him pull out the sandwich Julia had made, feeling very far away from her, as if her sandwich was a message sent long ago, when no one was trying to stick needles into anyone else.

"You know," said Hans as he watched Barry gleefully swallow his food, "I think he is the only happy one here."

# Congratulations! It's an Embryo

I FOLLOWED CHANTAL down a long corridor leading to the room I would masturbate in. In my right hand I held a brown paper bag, and in that bag was a container to hold my semen. Julia's eggs were ready and had just been collected. Now it was my turn.

One by one, the design features of the clinic tapered off: gone the blond-wood doors with their brushed metal handles, gone, too, the pinprick spotlights, the panelled walls, the potted floor plants. Just a long, bare corridor. The clinic had obviously spent most of its money out front, and for good reason – if you were this far in, they already had your business.

Chantal stopped in front of a door. She opened it.

"Here we go," she said.

I peered inside. In the far corner of the narrow room was a chair. Opposite the chair, a small table with a stack of pornographic magazines, highlighted by the bank of fluorescent ceiling panels. To my immediate right was a sink. On the sink stand was a bottle of pump soap and an aerosol can of Lysol disinfectant. It was a large can, industrial-sized, the kind you place under the kitchen sink and used if you had a lot of pets in the house, or cigar smokers.

"When you are finished, please place your sample in the bag and deposit it on the table behind me." Chantal stepped aside and allowed me to see a knee-high table with a red plastic in-basket found in any office supply store. "Be certain you've printed your name in legible letters and also the time of your sample. There is also a form. Please fill it out and staple it to your sample."

Chantal obligingly pointed to the stapler and a stack of forms sitting to the left of the in-basket and I nodded to let her know that I understood.

"You can go in now," Chantal said.

I retreated to my room and closed the door.

This room, with its blank, uncompromising, fluorescent meanness showed a rude, almost cynical disregard for my comfort. Dr. Henderson had probably never visited this part of his establishment. He'd left the decorating details to Chantal and the rest of the nursing staff, whose contempt was obvious. For example: the chair had armrests. This, I could immediately see, offered unwanted obstacles to the task at hand – someone had simply picked a chair up from the reception area, brought it here, and shoved it into a corner.

I sat on the chair, unfastened my pants, and lifted my bum in the air so I could pull them down. I suddenly thought of Tamara. It wasn't the right thing to do, thinking of Tamara.

Julia was lying on a hospital bed, wedged between locked safety bars, recuperating from the egg extraction. I'd been standing close by, holding her hand, when Chantal had pushed aside the privacy curtain and told me to follow her. Julia had turned to one side, brought her knees up toward her chest, and closed her eyes.

I'd been there when they'd taken her eggs; it seemed my attendance was a moral requirement, an expectation on behalf of the clinic and Julia that I would be beside her. I'd been seated on a padded stool, watching Julia position her feet in the stirrups. She looked pale and fragile, yet determined.

Beyond my wife's raised legs was Dr. Henderson. Until that moment I'd only seen him in his office, which was rather like only seeing pilots in airport terminals. He was prepping, checking, monitoring.

I sat on my little stool, which had no backrest and small wheels so that I was only the slightest push away from sliding toward the other side of the room.

"Okay," said Dr. Henderson.

Behind a low wall, the top half consisting of opened shutters, stood the lab technician – the doctor's co-pilot – swaddled in a blue medical gown, the lower part of his face covered by a surgical mask. Dr. Henderson was to retrieve the eggs, the lab technician, standing ten to fifteen feet away, to receive them. A very long, thin plastic umbilical cord snaked its way up from Dr. Henderson's hand to a hook on the ceiling, then fell back down into the hands of the assistant.

"Okay," the doctor repeated when he'd positioned himself behind the blue partition that separated Julia's lower body from her upper. I couldn't see anything, but expected a flinch of pain from Julia. She remained impassive. There was the faint whirl and beep of machines and then Dr. Henderson said, "Finished," first to the lab technician, who immediately closed the shutters on us. An assistant entered and wheeled Julia out of the room and into a small curtained area where she could rest. And wait.

Why was it so bright in here? Had no one thought of dimmers? Porno mags were piled in two stacks on the small corner table. Again, I thought of Tamara. I picked up a copy of *Honey Holes* and rested it on my bare knees. I started to do my business, but the armrests interfered.

I stood up. There was a light switch beside the sink. Clutching my open pants I shuffled over, turned off the light, and was immediately plunged into darkness. I blinked several times, waited for my eyes to adjust, but there was no light for my eyes to adjust to. I bent down. Surely some light must be seeping through the door but no, the door made a hermetic seal. Reaching out for the wall, which felt cool and solid, I traced my steps back to the chair, hit my knee, stumbled, sat down, and began to tug my penis urgently. My elbows banged against the armrests, so I stood up thinking, *Why sit down, I can do this standing up*. Then I sat down again.

How much time did I have, anyway? Not much. Julia's eggs were already *out*. "No room for failure," Dr. Henderson had pitilessly remarked, seconds after Julia was wheeled out of the operating room. His way of putting me at ease, I supposed. I knew what they did with bulls: they stuck a metal rod up their ass and fired off an electrical bolt. I redoubled my efforts.

When it was time, I leaned over, patted down the table, found the brown paper bag, retrieved the plastic vial, twisted off the cap. I couldn't see. I needed some light – it was a question of accuracy. I placed the vial back down on the table, stood up, reached out for the wall, and shuffled my way back toward the light switch, careful not to trip and fall over my unfastened pants. I would need to work quickly, with a certain imaginative efficiency. I located the light switch, picked up my pants, and ran myself back to the chair. I grabbed the vial. I positioned it. I stared at the sink and did my business.

The corridor was empty. I walked over to the in-basket; two other bags were already sitting in its shallow hold. I glanced at the other doors, a long line of them, stretching down the corridor. Behind each of them must have been a chair, a sink, a *Honey Holes* magazine, and an occupant.

I wrote my name in the bold, clear letters insisted upon by the nurse though I felt neither bold nor particularly clear. I printed out the time of sample: 10:10 a.m. Then I filled out the form: my name again, the name of my partner, my address, my phone number (home and office.) I stapled the form to my paper bag and dropped it into the plastic tray with the other two bags that looked as impotent and useless as my own.

Who picked them up? And when? Someone must have been ordered to make rounds, but it seemed like a lost world back here, a place where, if you decided to never emerge from your room, you'd be forgotten. Unlike the technological order out front, with its modern machines and medical gowns and stainless-steel stirrups, this was a world of dropped pants and paper bags.

I began my journey back toward Julia with a sense that my actions, my participation, were of no interest or account to anyone. My sperm would be collected by a person unseen, unknown, then scrutinized by Dr. Henderson's impersonal eye.

He'd be looking for a promising sperm, one to pluck from a cast of billions. His choice would determine my child. What if it was a monster? Or an idiot like Barry? It ought to have been my right – my duty – to make the selection.

The potted plants, the plush carpet, the directional lights, all returned as I joined the other men who milled about the curtained rooms that enveloped their wives. Several men had a certain glow about them, an aura, as if the activity that presently engaged them was infused with the divine: *We are in the act of procreation*. I wished they'd go away. The rest of the men, including myself, stood there, ashamed and dissatisfied that their wives were eggless and they themselves were useless.

I pulled open the curtain.

"How'd everything go?" Julia was sipping apple juice from a swivel straw. Two plump pillows propped up her back.

"Fine," I answered, bending forward and squeezing her hand. "Everything's just fine."

# Accidents Can Happen

AFTER THE CLINIC RELEASED US, I took Julia home and tucked her into bed. I turned down the blinds, admiring the effect of darkness upon the room, and brought her a glass of water, watched her take an impassive sip, then took the glass out of her hand and placed it on her bedside table. Julia wasn't sick; she wasn't even all that tired. The clinic hadn't thought it necessary she stay at home for the day. They were very sloppy about that sort of thing, I decided. Julia's eggs had been extracted from her body and surely that warranted some sort of time off: I'd insisted she come home with me and get under the covers.

"You need to rest," I said, sitting down beside her.

"What I need is to get away."

Julia took a moment to think about what she'd just said, then asked me to get her purse from downstairs. When I returned, I found her sitting cross-legged on the bed, clothed in a T-shirt pulled down to her knees. The shades had been opened, light poured into the room. She pulled out her wallet, picked up the phone, and recounted for me Dr. Henderson's description of Bermuda, its friendly people and pink-sanded beaches, the splendid golf courses.

"But we don't play golf," I reminded her.

"It's less than a three-hour flight," she said, dialling a number printed on the back of her frequent-flyer card. "We have enough points."

A great number of those points had been accumulated by purchasing the fertility drugs on frequent-mile credit cards, just as Dr. Henderson suggested, and just as I had complied not too long ago at the discount pharmacy when Barry had farted in the car. Every one of those points represented an accumulation of failure, though I hoped Julia didn't see it that way.

"I want to go," she said, cradling the phone between her shoulder and chin.

"When?"

"Two or three days after our next appointment at the clinic. Let's say two. Wednesday."

Our next appointment at the clinic was to insert the fertilized eggs into Julia's body. They'd retrieved ten of them, not a bad number, the doctor had told us. Right now they were cloistered in some sort of incubator that kept them warm and comfortable. Hopefully, they would begin to divide and divide again. They would be graded, like common farm eggs, and, in about three days, depending on how things were going, only the better few would be put back where they belonged, inside Julia. Then all of us would wing our way to sunny Bermuda.

"It's a bit sudden," I said. *It's a bit frantic*, I thought.

"I need to go."

Julia spoke to someone from reservations, who checked for availability.

"They might not have any seats," I said.

They had seats.

"Julia, it's crazy, we can't just drop everything and take off."

"Why not? I've been thinking about doing this for a while."

"But I haven't."

"You said you wanted me to rest."

"In bed, here, in our own home."

"I'm feeling fucked up. Luke, I need to do this."

I noticed Julia hadn't cupped the receiver with her hand. She didn't care, as a Riddell was supposed to care, that she'd exposed our domestic problems to a complete stranger, who was at this precise moment listening on the other end of the phone, making judgments.

"Why don't you put the phone down and we'll talk about it?"

But Julia didn't put the phone down. "You're acting like I'm booking tickets to hell," she said. "It's Bermuda! And you're wrong that we can't just go. Of course we can. And I refuse to sit around in this bed with the blinds closed hoping I'm pregnant."

I shut my eyes and saw the possibility of her doing precisely that. "Book me a window seat," I said.

It was just past one when I drove back to the bird factory. The highway was free of rush-hour commuters and the billboards, without spectators, were like television sets left on in empty houses. I no longer had a clear idea if I'd meant to go to the factory today or if I'd planned to stay home with Julia, but I'd left shortly after she started looking for hotels on the Internet.

I'd given Barry the day off. The afternoon before, when I'd brought him back to his residence, I'd paid him his wages, which had been given to me by his father, and told him to spend the day with Christy. Lloyd Riddell had asked me what I knew of Barry's affections toward her. I told him I knew nothing except that Christy was there every morning when I came to pick Barry up and was there every evening when I dropped him off, but that I had no idea what happened in the hours in between. My remarks had done little to satisfy Lloyd, who reluctantly handed me the money for his son as if I hadn't earned my pay.

*Fuck him*, I thought. I'd just masturbated into a plastic cup; I had my own problems. I didn't want to spy on Barry, I hadn't wanted to hire him, and I didn't like driving him to and from work every day. At the factory, Barry talked to Tamara, and he listened to Philip, whose natural patience he instantly responded to. And that, as far as I was concerned, was as far as it was going to get.

It was Julia's fault, somehow, that I was caught up in all this. Roger was her fault too. I hadn't wanted either one of them at the factory, nor did I want to go to Bermuda. I didn't seem to be in control, not of my sperm, not of our airline points, not my privacy, not even the bird factory. I pulled into the parking lot and saw Tamara's yellow BABY ON BOARD! sticker on her back car window. I hit the brakes and stared at the words, so simple, a statement of fact, yet menacing too. BABY ON BOARD! That yellow sticker was forever just a few feet in front of Julia and me, both a warning not to approach too close and a promise; it was something that we would follow, chase after, from clinics to beaches to bed.

Jamaican dancehall was blaring out of the speakers when I walked in to the factory. Tamara was bent over the counter reading a magazine, shaking her ass, seemingly oblivious to my presence. She was wearing white track pants with the waistband turned down, and thong underwear.

Without Barry around, I found myself gazing at Tamara free of inhibitions. The knots in her taut spine retreated when she stretched herself out and turned around.

"I can feel you looking at me."

A small finger-stroke of paint covered her lower lip. I couldn't take my eyes off the glittering colour.

"Hard at work?" I asked.

Tamara didn't seem the least embarrassed by her lack of productivity or the fact I'd been staring at her. She was smiling and dancing like that was the job she'd been paid to do.

"I've only been trying to call you for, like, the past three years," she said, and pointed to the untouched heap of wings and bird bodies that were piled up just beyond the open pages of her magazine. "We're out of bird string or whatever you call it. I looked around but couldn't find anything so I tried to do some painting."

"Don't worry about it," I said. "At least someone's enjoying themselves today."

"Where have you been anyway?"

"Errands."

"Didn't you check your messages?"

"No," I said, remembering that I'd turned my cellphone off at the clinic; it was possible Tamara had been trying to call while I'd been in the room with *Honey Holes* magazine, thinking about her. I turned the music down.

"My parents don't let me play it loud in the house." Tamara rolled her eyes. "Things are pretty tense over there."

"Things are pretty tense at home for me too," I said.

Tamara leaned over and turned the music back up. "Sounds like we could both use a little fun."

Fun sounded good, I thought. We weren't going to make any birds today. Philip had taken the day off to work on his house, Roger was out scouting for his latest addition – a fingerprint ID reader that I had absolutely no use for, but which he insisted was a valuable "security asset" – Hans had worked the day before and Barry was back at the residence, probably having sex with Christy.

Tamara and I were alone. When I'd left the house, had I known there'd only be the two of us? Tamara danced her way into the next room, where Philip usually worked, and pulled on the ribbons dangling from all the birds, setting them in flight, their bodies rising and falling with each pulsating beat of their wings, exactly as Julia had done that first day when she'd stepped into the factory, laughing because, in her words, she'd "stepped into the sky."

The car keys were still in my hand, warmed by the heat of my enclosed palm. I knew I should get into my car and drive away, drive home, drive anywhere.

"I'm going," I said, breaking for the front door.

"Where?" Tamara called out, surprised.

"I don't know."

It was raining when I stepped outside. I saw Mr. Chang, standing close against the wall of his premises, clipboard in hand as if to record my movements. I rushed for the car without waving, opened the door, and sat inside, watching the rain wash down the windows. I took a few deep breaths, flipped open my phone, and called Julia to see how she was, to see how *I* was. I imagined she'd still be researching Bermuda on the Internet, but she wasn't. "I'm climbing the walls," she said and all at once started to cry. "Sorry, the drugs." I told her to get some rest and, feeling ashamed by my impatience, hung up.

Going home wasn't an option. I turned on the ignition and idled. *That's all I've ever been doing*, I thought, *idling, waiting, never putting my foot down on the accelerator*. I didn't have lazy sperm; I *was* lazy sperm. Enclosed by the waterfall of rain cascading down the windows, I felt trapped and restless, desperate to move but mesmerized and held by the flowing, beating water. Inside the factory, only a few feet away, Tamara was prancing about in thong underwear, music blaring, birds flapping.

Fun. Sex. When was the last time I'd been able to slip into those short, lean words? I'd been fattened up with Julia's sorrows and my own inexcusable failure. I was obese. The only words I could fit into were tailored extra large, the kind found at the back of the store in the "relaxed fit" section: procreation, fatherhood, fertility.

I turned the engine off, pulled out my key, and ran past Mr. Chang again, heading for the factory, the swaying birds, and Tamara. I was thinking of the way Barry reached for Christy when I leaned in and kissed her. Her lips tasted like waxy lipgloss. My approach, so rapid and unexpected, took her off guard; I reached under her shirt and ran my fingers along her smooth skin.

"Hey," said Tamara. "Stop." She tugged on my hair, forcing me to look at her. "What are you doing?"

I refused to meet her eyes; instead I let my gaze wander down past her breasts to her belly button, a perfect fleshy dot, the marked centre of her body, so close and accessible. "I'm having fun," I said, breaking free of her grip. I dropped down on my knees and swirled my tongue around her belly button as if it was the last lick of a lollipop, then I slipped my fingers under the waistband of her white track pants and tried to pull them down. "Luke!" Tamara shouted. She grabbed hold of her pants and I froze. In a much softer tone, Tamara said, "You're married."

With my head still pressed against her belly, I had the impression that, if I'd wanted to, Tamara would have let me suck her belly button for a while longer, just to calm me down. I could see myself through her eyes – a married man on his knees trying to have sex with his younger employee.

I stood up and turned away as Tamara readjusted her clothes. There, in the next room, was Julia's peacock feather, recently dusted, a clear blue eye staring at me.

"I'm going to move in with Philip when he's finished the house," Tamara said. "I need someone who's stable. Someone like Philip."

"He's a good man." It sounded silly, expressed that way, and in these circumstances, but it was true, Philip *was* a good man, kind and patient, good with Barry and Tamara's children, and capable of building his own house.

I stepped back out into the rain and, in short little hops across the puddles, ran back to the car, pulled out of the parking lot, and headed for home.

# Chaos Theory

DUNCAN SAT AT THE HEAD OF HIS TABLE, knife and fork in hand, as if anticipating the need to carve up the table itself, and concentrated his attention on a small patch of chicken on my plate. He looked mean and small and distrustful.

"Your father's an idiot," my mother said.

Since I'd last seen her, Emily had brightened her clothes and her hair and her fingernails. She looked like an embassy flag fluttering over hostile territory.

I carved the meat – more white for Julia, legs and wings for Duncan and me. Nothing for my mother. "What's wrong with you?" she said. "Can't you even find a student in someone else's class?"

Duncan, out of some atavistic survival technique, remained utterly motionless, as if he knew any movement would alert potential prey to his position. I continued to carve through the chicken; my mother scooped some rice onto her plate. There was a moment, just a brief, blissful moment, when all the domestic graces were observed. But it didn't last.

"You know what your problem is? You're a coward! Only cowards do what you've done. You don't have any balls."

"But the problem is I do." These were Duncan's first words and they were the wrong ones.

"Duncan! This isn't the nineteen-seventies. You can't just fuck your students and get them pregnant!

"I didn't know you could do that in the nineteen-seventies either." My father seemed pleased by his dry remark, which of course only made my mother angrier.

"The university will fire you if they find out, Duncan. They might even press charges. You can't imagine how hysterical everyone is about these things nowadays."

For all my mother's anger, I was not unaware that her concern seemed to focus on Duncan's position at the university.

Duncan said, "Rosemary," and patted his lips with a napkin as if her name was some unwanted moisture he wished to blot away. "Her name is Rosemary."

Emily turned to look at me with an expression I hadn't seen since I was a child, the one that said she would soon be forced to abandon me for a while, and I felt myself shrinking in my chair, becoming smaller and smaller, until every object in the room took on the seemingly impassable massiveness of childhood.

"I've made a very upsetting discovery tonight," my mother said.

*Obviously*, I thought.

Whatever my mother had found out about Duncan and Rosemary, I hoped it didn't include my accidental meeting with Rosemary at The Steak House. I'd been trying to keep my distance from my parents for weeks to avoid getting pulled further into things, but Julia had ambushed me by accepting my mother's dinner invitation for the evening before our trip to Bermuda. I hadn't said a word about Rosemary to my mother and I'd kept it a secret from Julia as well, a less forgivable action somehow: what happened between Duncan and my mother was their affair, what happened between Julia and me was mine.

I played dumb.

"What's he done now?" I asked.

"Your idiot father has had an affair with one of his students. And now she's pregnant and is insisting on having the child. He didn't have the courage to deal with it himself, so he came to me, told me everything, and asked if I'd talk to her."

I shook my head in disbelief. It was bad enough what Duncan had done, but to ask my mother to intervene? It was unconscionable. And yet I was no longer in a position to condemn him – if Tamara hadn't pushed me away that afternoon at the factory, I would have slept with her, and somehow that fact, that I'd tried, paid the price, morally speaking, yet failed, made what I'd done feel all that much worse.

"And so that's just what I did," my mother continued. "I've been in contact with Rosemary for the past month."

"You've known for the past month?" I'd spoken to my mother over the phone in the last few weeks – there was no avoiding her completely – and there'd been nothing in her voice, nothing at all, to warn me. "Then why are you so upset now?" I asked, astonished, as always, by my parents' relationship.

"I'll tell you why! This morning I was cleaning up your father's desk and I found an outline, a paper edit, of a film he's been shooting. Your father is making a documentary of Rosemary's pregnancy."

"Don't exaggerate," said Duncan. "You weren't cleaning, you were snooping."

"I called Rosemary and she told me it's true, you're filming her." Emily yelled, "You are a coward! A coward for doing this! In fifteen years, the only film you can make is one documenting your own mess. You are nothing more than a dog lapping up its own vomit!"

Duncan coughed into his hand, then folded his arms. He said nothing.

"Can you imagine what would happen if this ever got out? Rosemary's a very confused young woman. After all the work I've put in to calming the situation down, who knows how this will affect her."

My mother should have left Duncan years ago but had elected to remain behind to torment him instead. And like any task successfully completed, she'd gained a rising confidence over the years. I looked at Julia to see how she was doing. She'd hardly said a word since we'd arrived at the house. It must have been shocking for her, as a Riddell, to hear what the Grays were capable of. But as I turned toward her to offer support, I saw that she was, instead, looking at me with an expression almost identical to the one my mother had given me moments before, like I was on the verge of being abandoned.

And then I understood.

"How long have you known about Rosemary?" I asked.

My teeth began to hurt. Very distinct, very sharp, as if I'd crunched down on tinfoil with a mouth full of cavities. I wanted to scream.

"From the beginning."

"Why are you involved in this!" I shouted.

But it seemed so obvious to me now. I was amazed I'd missed it. Julia, in her work and in her life, wasn't someone who managed crises, she was someone who thrived on them. There'd been a hidden battle between us, between order and chaos, and chaos had won. She was more like my family than I'd ever realized.

"She's been very helpful to Rosemary," said my mother.

To my astonishment, Duncan nodded.

"I wanted to help," Julia said.

"But these people are *unhelpable*. Don't you understand that?"

My mother accepted the insult. "But Rosemary isn't," she said. "What happened to her . . . it wasn't her fault."

"It's not mine either. Or Julia's."

"Her family lives out east," Julia interrupted. "She isn't going to tell them. She can't. I'm closer to her age than your mother."

"And, conveniently, you're not the wife of the man who impregnated her."

With those words, the impregnating man in question stood up and wandered away from the dining-room table. No one stopped him. Yet we all observed his silent retreat.

I expected him to go upstairs, but instead I heard him open the basement door.

"I hope he never comes back up," my mother said.

"There's no helping this family," I said.

"You *are* this family," Julia answered.

She was right, of course. And so I stood up. My father was a fool and a failure and now it was my turn to join him.

After he built the river, Duncan had proclaimed his marriage to be "open" as if he were an incompetent locksmith who couldn't – or wouldn't – secure the doors from outside intruders. I'd witnessed the shock and hurt and shame my mother had suffered from that first day when we'd seen Duncan tucked beneath the waterfall, baptizing himself into the beliefs he'd so loudly proclaimed, but I'd also seen the outcome of her absence and her suffering on Duncan. The choices he'd made for himself had led directly to his own diminishment. It was my father's sense of loss, of abandonment, that saddened me beyond anything previously imaginable.

I opened the door to the basement, walked down the stairs, and stood beside my father on what had once been a riverbed.

"I tried to sleep with an employee."

Duncan raised an imaginary wineglass. "To the Grays," he said, "a colour that best describes its men."

His tone was meant to be mocking but sounded, instead, sadly meaningful. I took a deep breath. Duncan joined me and together we let out a long, hollow sigh.

"I would have slept with her," I said. "That's the worst of it. I would have slept with her if she hadn't pushed me away."

"Why'd she do that?" my father asked.

I shrugged, not wanting to acknowledge that she was a more decent person than I was, and looked up at the white cylindrical spotlights, the only thing left untouched by the flood. Once so properly modern, they now looked like abandoned insect nests.

"Just wondering," Duncan asked, "but if you had managed to sleep with her, would you have used a condom? Did you have one with you?"

"No."

"You see, it isn't so easy to plan ahead, is it?"

"Not for us," I admitted morosely, imagining that if I'd caught some sort of disease – gonorrhea, syphilis, chlamydia – I still wouldn't be able to tell Dr. Henderson what was what. *She might have even become pregnant*, I thought. It was possible, wasn't it? The notion momentarily and unexpectedly lifted my spirits. *That would show them*, I said to myself. It wasn't until I sauntered over to one of the dark corners of the basement, pried open a loose brick, reached in and pulled out a packet of ancient cigarettes that I wondered what it was, exactly, I wished to show, or even whom I wished to show it to.

"Remember the river?" Duncan asked, accepting a cigarette. "I think I've always wanted to escape from myself. Back then everything seemed so possible, so permissible, even my own success."

It was a habit of my father to slip into self-pity whenever he felt threatened or unhappy. The problem, as I saw it, was that our concerns were of a more immediate nature.

"Why is my wife visiting your pregnant student?" *Why*, I wondered, *must my fate be so closely touched by your own?*

"She likes to help people, your wife. I guess that's why she married you."

We each had a cigarette dangling from our lips before realizing we were without matches. I walked into the furnace room and lit my cigarette from the furnace's pilot light, just as I'd done as a teenager.

"We'll go up after we finish," Duncan said when I returned.

*No, we wouldn't*, I thought. We were stuck in this goddamn basement, the place I'd never left, would never leave, my past, my present, my future.

# Off Course

JULIA AND I FLEW TO BERMUDA. Though the sky was clear when we arrived, the sea was frothing in anger. At our hotel, the woman behind the check-in counter told us we probably had only a day or two to enjoy ourselves before a Category One hurricane, swirling up from the Caribbean, hit the island. An omen, I thought, and of the worst kind. "There are only two sorts of people who like storms, surfers and bird-watchers," she said, handing over our room keys. I'd already spotted the surfers, riding their waves onto battered shores.

The hotel Julia had picked for us, probably while I'd been on my knees sucking Tamara's belly button, was, as its promotional literature so proudly boasted, the tallest building on the highest point of land in all Bermuda; it dominated the surrounding countryside, which, from what I could tell from our eighth-floor balcony, consisted primarily of a golf course that meandered in manicured perfection all the way down to the sea. We changed quickly for the beach and found that we needed to board a tram; evidently the hotel's preference for commanding heights outweighed its decision to locate on the water. The passengers, dressed in sandals and shorts, baseball caps, and candy-coloured T-shirts, looked like prematurely aged children as they held on to the safety straps.

There weren't many people on the beach that afternoon. The tennis courts were empty, as were most of the tables beside the snack bar. "It's October. All the kids are back at school and it's too early for the holidays," Julia said. I couldn't be sure what significance, if any, these words held for her, but as Julia recounted the obvious advantages of travelling off-season – clean beaches, cheaper hotel rates, no crowds – I couldn't help surveying the beach and taking its emptiness in a personal way.

Newspapers were scattered about the beach, pages fluttering in the breeze, their owners perhaps fled in terror. They were full of news about the storm, its wind speed and direction, its origins and potential destruction. From the comfort of my beach chair I read an article that suggested global warming might be responsible; humankind, it speculated, was changing the world, making it more unstable and threatening. I felt this way about Julia, who had indolently stretched herself out on the hot sand a few feet away from me.

"Can you believe we have almost the whole beach to ourselves?" she said.

"Maybe everyone's avoiding us."

Julia, frowning, rolled over on her belly and closed her eyes.

Putting my paper aside to stare at her, I thought I could see the exhaustion on her back, which seemed to have lost its shape, its personality – the winged protrusions of her shoulder blades, the indentation of her stitching spine, and the narrowing of her waist was now just flat and formless. It belonged to a person I no longer recognized.

"Why are you staring at me?" Julia asked.

"I'm not," I said, startled, because Julia's eyes were still closed, and because I'd been, without quite realizing it, unfavourably comparing my wife's back to Tamara's.

"You're wound up, Luke. Try to relax."

I decided to get some drinks. A bartender, dressed in Bermuda shorts and running shoes, walked over the groomed sand and took my order.

"Here's to being here," Julia said when he returned with our plastic cups. I picked up my rum and Coke and took a sip without saying a word. "I'm glad we came," she said, "even if there is a storm. It's good to get out of Toronto." Julia handed me a tube of suntan lotion. "Would you rub some onto my shoulders?"

I ordered another drink and leaned down beside her, pressing my thumbs into her tired muscles. "God that feels good," Julia groaned.

Julia had worked late at the office every night for the past week, including the day she'd gone to the clinic to receive her three fertilized eggs. Even so, she'd taken her computer with her on the plane to Bermuda. It never ended for her. She was always busy – with work, with my family, with having a family. It would never end. As for me, I hadn't been back to the bird factory since peeling off in the car park. My transgression with Tamara already seemed faded and hardly possible, yet I felt that way about my marriage too.

"Don't forget my legs," Julia said, kicking the air.

When I finished rubbing the lotion into her skin, Julia warned me to do the same. "Do you want me to put some on you?" she asked, concerned by my exposure to the sun. I shook my head and retreated beneath the shade of my umbrella, where I lay on my back and stared up at the thousands of minute perforations in the fabric and thought to myself how hard it is to block things out.

I turned onto my stomach and shut my eyes. *Relax. Let it drop away.* I'd phoned Philip, to put him in charge while I was gone, but it was a perfunctory call, because more and more Philip was in charge whether I was there or not. The bird factory ran itself, or rather Philip ran it for me. We made birds, we shipped them to stores, people bought them. Simple.

The next day we rented mopeds to explore the island and escape our own thoughts. Julia rode out front, a bulbous white helmet attached to her head like a distended ovary that had grown riotously in the subtropical heat. Workmen, readying the island for the incoming storm, raised tanned arms in the direction of Julia's summer dress.

We passed pastel-coloured towns, pink-sanded beaches, and everywhere flowering gardens. Bermuda was the sort of place where tragedy and disorder had been thoughtfully brushed beneath carpets of sand and grass. As the brochures tirelessly pointed out, Bermuda was shaped like a fishhook – a curved spit of land that hadn't caught anything interesting for a very long time.

"It's great here," Julia hollered as I overtook her on the road.

The three eggs had been inserted into her body only a few mornings ago, each one a potential life that, in this unnatural break of seasons, might eventually make its way into the world. Meanwhile, we were supposed to be on vacation, so later that evening we decided to treat ourselves and go out for a nice dinner. Julia preferred to walk rather than take the mopeds to the restaurant. The air was warm, with a pleasant, soft breeze; yet I could locate neither joy, nor excitement, nor enthusiasm within me, and I felt old because of it. Julia, meanwhile, kept looking up at the stars. Her hope was monstrous, it consumed the universe.

Because of the stars, Julia wanted to eat outside, but the patio was closed, perhaps because of the storm, perhaps because the people of Bermuda, or the tourists who visited the island, thought it wiser to chill themselves with air conditioning. The tuxedo-clad maître d' led us to our table and handed us two oversized menus bound by a gold ribbon. The restaurant, with its flag-stone columns and three-tiered water fountain that perfumed the air with chlorine mist, was 1970s Malibu on the outside, yet inside it was furnished like a British men's club, all wood panelling and heavy furniture, with oil paintings of fox hunters and show horses. I was thinking that the confusion of styles was not unlike Julia and me, when she suddenly snapped the menu shut. "That's enough, Luke."

"Enough what?"

"You're just sitting there, glowering. Stop being so angry with me. What your father did is not my fault, Rosemary having his baby is not my fault, your mother asking for my help is not my fault. What *is* my fault is not telling you about it. But now you know." Julia looked around at the tables, most of them vacant. "There are worse places to be than Bermuda."

I shrugged. *The worst place to be*, I thought, *is wherever we are*.

The next morning I saw, from my hotel balcony, the first great line of brooding clouds, stretching from sea to sky, waiting offshore like a disciplined army ready to pounce. If Julia didn't get pregnant this time around, I knew we would have to try again. Again and again and again.

Julia wanted to get to the beach before the storm hit. I forgot how much she loved the water and watched her attack the incoming waves, diving beneath them, her bum the last thing I'd see before she'd pop up on the other side.

When she returned to the beach, her skin dripping with ocean water, she picked up her towel, rubbed her hair dry, then lay down on the sand. She wore a green, one-piece bathing suit that glistened in the sun before slowly fading as the fabric dried out in the hot air.

"What if you don't become pregnant?" I asked.

Julia winced, as if the glaring sun suddenly burned her face. "That's a terrible thing to say to me right now."

"I know, but it won't change the outcome."

"We'll keep trying."

"Julia, I'm not sure I want children that much."

"I've already apologized for what I've done."

"I'm not saying this out of anger."

"Yes, you are. You've been angry ever since we got here, before we got here. You've hardly said a word. You sit on the beach reading about the storm, or stand on the balcony looking for it. I think you want it to come."

"If we'd just *had* them, then I suppose . . ." I stopped myself, knowing how ugly I sounded. Why was I tormenting her? *Let her be.*

"You've changed things," I said. "I just want everything to be normal."

Julia leapt up from her towel. "Having a baby *is* normal. Even this way. There is no perfect world, Luke, no perfect person who's going to make sense of it for you. My father drinks and my mother just wants to redesign the table he puts his glass on. They've never really accepted the fact that their son is retarded. There's no such thing as normal."

Julia grabbed her things and marched back to the tram stop.

Later, when we got to the room, Julia turned on the television and selected an inane movie intended for an audience no older than fourteen. I felt she'd chosen it purposely to annoy me and went out to the balcony, closing the sliding door behind me to muffle Julia's outbursts of laughter. The storm still lay out to sea, hovering, waiting, but it did not come in. The sky became overcast, the air humid, almost fetid. I took a walk around the hotel grounds, but returned in less than half an hour.

And still the storm did not come.

I lay down on the bed and draped an arm over my eyes. I think I fell asleep. I turned on my side, then the other, then back again. Julia sat at the corner table, playing solitaire, card on top of card; a quick, perfunctory shuffle and it began all over again. She seemed to age in front of me, getting older and older with every beat of my heart, a lighted candle on her table casting bruised shadows in the hollow of her cheeks; and then

Julia was poking at my shoulder and I opened my eyes, expecting to see her hunched over the table but finding instead that her body was curled around my own.

"You've seen those women in the waiting room. They're so pathetic, sitting there in business suits, desperate. Like me."

It was only then that I heard the wind, and the rain, hurling itself against our hotel room, eight floors above ground, as if trying to pry off anything not securely fastened down.

I rolled over and faced her.

"You're not pathetic," I said. "I am."

Julia leaned in, close enough for her lips to brush against my cheeks.

"I've thought of leaving you." I had to fight the wind, compete against it, to hear her. "Have you ever thought of leaving me?"

"I don't know, maybe," I answered. "We've messed things up."

And for the first time in a long while we made love with something like passion and interest and abandon: we made love for its own sake.

When I woke up, Julia was standing beside the open shutters. Sunlight flooded the room. Where, seemingly moments before, howling winds and heavy rain had promised irreparable damage, everything was now bathed in a soft, powdery light. I took Julia's hand as we stepped out onto the balcony, surveying the fresh, new land below. A voice from the balcony next door called out to us. Beyond the partition, Julia and I could see a man's arm, extended over the railing, a gnarled finger pointing to the golf course.

"Look!" the man said. "Do you see the bobolinks?"

We confessed that we did not.

"Look!" he said again, this time handing us his binoculars from around the partition.

Julia and I did our best to feign interest, not knowing what we were looking for, when all at once I saw the flecked yellow land move. It was a carpet woven from exhausted, yellow-plumed birds.

"See them now?" The man asked, hearing my astonished gasp. "They've been blown off-course, thousands of them. Hell of a storm."

They were in the trees, on roofs and garden walls. Most were too exhausted to even flutter a fearful wing against us as Julia and I, after having thanked our bird-watching neighbour, walked down the road leading to the sea. There were people on the road, smiling and helpful, moving debris and offering assistance to anyone that might need it. We passed the restaurant we'd eaten in two nights before and were gratified to see that part of the patio overhang had been blown off, causing damage to the roof.

The few bobolinks strong enough to fly glided from side to side in the air, moving neither forward nor backward. Looking at them, I wondered why leaving Julia had never been an option in my mind. I could have packed my bags and just walked away from this mess. Perhaps I was like my mother that way: you stuck it out, no matter what, if only to plague and harass your partner.

Standing here, at the edge of a sea still churned and opaque from the storm, Julia's soft puddle of a hand in my own, it occurred to me that she could have had an affair herself but it didn't seem to bother me. I could accept it as punishment.

Julia suddenly withdrew her hand and pressed it sharply against her belly.

"I don't feel well," she said, bending over with a grimace.

I took her arm.

"What's wrong?"

"I don't know. It hurts."

Julia and I quickly returned to the hotel, her face pale. She was out of breath when I put her into bed and pulled the covers over her. When she was settled in, I walked out to the balcony. The exhausted bobolinks were still thick on the ground. The wind was picking up, the sky darkening. I could see a tremendous distance.

"I think another storm is coming," I called out, but Julia, rolling on her side so she could peer out the window replied, "Maybe it's just the same one."

# How It Ended

I RETURNED TO THE FACTORY to find that Hans had been fired. Not by me, because I'd been in Bermuda, but by Philip, who'd caught him stealing.

"I came in late one night because I wasn't sure Tamara had unplugged the glue guns," Philip explained, "and I saw him walking out the front door with paint and wood, rope, brushes, everything!"

"Are you sure he was stealing it?" I didn't put it past Hans to steal from us, but I was angry Philip had fired him without consulting me. "Maybe you misunderstood."

"He was carrying everything out in a shopping cart. And he didn't even deny what he was doing!"

"So you fired him on the spot? The thing is, Philip, if anyone is going to fire anybody in this company it should be me."

After the natural light of Bermuda, the fluorescent lights were giving me a headache and making Philip look unwell, though, in truth of fact, he looked better than he normally did. I peered at him closely.

"You get a haircut or something?"

Philip blushed, and then shook his head like a dog coming out of the water, in a failed attempt to return his hair to its once previous disorder. Then I noticed how bright his teeth were. I couldn't tell if his new-found looks were the cause or the effect of firing Hans, but I sensed defiance in him. I was still examining Philip's physical improvements – the closer shave, the neat sideburns, the awakened eyes – when he said, "Tamara and I are seeing each other."

It was a bit strange to hear it from Philip, so soon after my own arrested efforts with Tamara. It was just over *there* – I looked and marked the spot – that I'd been on my knees. I wondered if Philip was merely informing me that he was seeing Tamara or warning me.

"That's great," I said.

"She comes over to the trailer a lot."

"The kids too?"

Philip nodded. "I like them. And it's just for another six weeks or so. Then we're all going to move into the house together."

"Well, it looks like you got everything you wanted."

Pleased, Philip beamed his Crest-bright teeth at me.

Julia still wasn't feeling well after we returned from Bermuda. She saw it as a positive sign.

"My boobs are sore," she said, cupping her hands under her breasts and lifting them up to better experience their tenderness.

Whatever else it was that she felt sent her to the bathroom several times during the night. Julia may have been optimistic that she was pregnant, but it worried me that she was short of breath walking up stairs and that her belly hadn't stopped aching since Bermuda.

"Are you sure you're okay?" I asked after her third visit to the bathroom one night. Each time Julia returned to bed she curled her body around mine, and each time her body seemed just a little colder. After Bermuda, the city and everything in it seemed stripped of colour, Julia included.

"I'm fine," Julia murmured.

In my half-dreams I saw Philip's teeth, gleaming white like freshly painted seagulls, and felt an unshakable sense of foreboding. I opened my eyes and looked at the clock. It was just past three in the morning. Julia was breathing loudly and kept digging her knee into the back of my legs as if there was a slot she kept missing. It was uncomfortable under the covers with Julia's body pressed up against me, but I didn't want to move for fear I'd disturb whatever sleep she might be getting. If I turned around, I'd see how remarkably beautiful she was. I'd somehow forgotten that. I'd forgotten a lot of things.

In some ways Philip was lucky; his family was coming to him ready-made. He wouldn't have to lie in bed, staring at the illuminated dials of a clock, wondering if his wife was sick or pregnant or both. Actually, I thought my wife was sick. I didn't share Julia's optimism; and I felt my suspicions were disloyal.

Imagine if Julia had two children from a previous relationship? I'd have run. I felt like running now, away from Julia's enveloping arms, her heavy breathing. It struck me that we were supposed to grow old together in this bed, but now it seemed rather pointless, even tedious, without children.

Julia reached out with a clammy hand.

"Take me to the hospital."

I looked over at the clock.

"What's wrong?"

"Everything."

The machines and tubes hooked up to Julia's body were no longer in the service of creating a life, but of protecting one. There were real doctors this time – nurses too – who I felt had earned their white coats, their sternly practical indifference, and their diminutive jokes, made to relieve the tension.

When we'd arrived at Emergency, Julia had immediately informed the hospital that she'd been taking fertility drugs, as the clinic had warned her to do if she ever found herself in a situation like the one we were in. They had her on a gurney, IV in her arm, within minutes, and as I watched her get promptly whisked down the hospital corridor, I understood that this moment was what Julia had feared. She'd known all along that things weren't right.

An hour or so later, the attending physician came and spoke with me. Julia was suffering from OHSS, Ovarian Hyper Stimulation Syndrome. She had ovarian enlargement, high estrogen levels, fluid imbalances, and fluid accumulation in her abdomen, which they'd already begun to drain. The syndrome was fairly rare but further complicated if the patient was pregnant.

"She's pregnant?"

"There was no chance," the doctor interrupted, before I could ask the next part of the question. And from what he said next, it didn't look like there would be a chance again. Julia was very sick and, medically, would put herself at great risk if this syndrome flared a second time.

"She must have been in great discomfort for the past few days," the doctor said, and he asked why she hadn't admitted herself to the hospital at the first sign of trouble. *Because she was pregnant*, I wanted to say, *because to her the pain felt good.*

Afterwards, the doctor took me to see Julia, and I had a quiet moment with her just before she fell asleep. They'd given her some drugs for the pain and her eyes were glassy. She was too weak to plump her own pillow. I lifted her head – it felt remarkably heavy – and propped one pillow over the next so she could sit upright and look at me.

"I could probably try again."

As calmly as I could, I said, "Do you think that's wise?"

"No."

Julia's lips, weakened by the dry, institutional air of the hospital, had become, in just a few short hours, chapped and mauve-coloured. She licked them deliberately, like a lioness attending a wound. "I guess that's it."

"I guess it is. I'm so sorry, Julia."

"I'm sorry too."

She closed her eyes as the tears began to escape, and for once I knew what to do. I stroked her hair and whispered how much I loved her until she cried herself to sleep. When I returned home that morning, I found myself inspecting her bedside table: a bottle of skin cream; a silver bracelet – one of

Julia's favourites, with little half-moons and smiling suns; an assortment of earrings, some of them unpaired. There was something comforting about all these items, as if they assured Julia's return. Although the doctors said the mortality rate of OHSS was extremely low, it was life-threatening, and Julia had to be closely monitored. The doctors had to calm her body down, soothe and deflate it; in short, Julia had to become a Riddell once more.

A sense of my initial fright came back to me – Julia doubling over as she got out of bed, the panicked drive to the hospital, the doors of Emergency slitting open like a wound. There was so much of her here, in this house, so many of her possessions, so many of mine, that it seemed impossible they could ever be untangled. I switched off her bedside lamp because it was already light outside and, though it was just past seven, called her parents. They had to know; it was my duty to tell them. Mr. Riddell picked up the phone.

"Julia's in the hospital," I said.

"What's wrong with her?"

And so I told him. Without quite realizing it, I had imagined myself having this conversation with Maureen, because Maureen usually answered the phone, and because it seemed that the sort of things I now had to say were best said to a mother. I'd prepared myself for questions and worried interjections; instead, I had Lloyd Riddell on the line. Confronted with his silence, I said too much. I told him about the fertility treatments, about the drugs and my lazy sperm, but mostly I told him about Julia. How she was in the hospital and wanted babies and couldn't have them.

When Lloyd finally spoke, it was to ask one practical question. "What hospital is she in?" I answered, and he hung up.

At the hospital, Lloyd took quick, disputatious action, moving his daughter from a semi-private room to a private one. In the sartorial display of an ex-banker, he captained his way down hospital corridors with the surveying eye of a shareholder, while Barry, who no longer had a lift to the bird factory, followed close behind, in the wake of his father's authority.

If the private room was an improvement, it was still a bare and coldly functional room, with light green walls and a chipped metal bed that greatly offended Maureen Riddell's design philosophy. She immediately outfitted the room with cotton cozies over the door handles (she'd heard door handles in hospitals were stealthy transmitters of infection), draped several sarongs over the heating grill, and placed fluffy towels over the invalid bars in the bathroom. She filled the room with flowers.

Her assistance was, like her husband's, practical, functional, and useful. The Riddells offered everything they could and I'd come to see that it was not enough. All my life I'd fantasized that a family like theirs would steal me away from Emily and Duncan, pluck the dirty, disgraceful feathers off my back and send me out, clean and washed and initiated into the ways of leading a proper life; but here, at this seminal moment, they couldn't bring themselves to talk about what had happened. Lloyd never mentioned our conversation again; incredibly, neither did Maureen, who seemed to be content with whatever Lloyd had told her. She preferred to bustle about the room, trying to make it pretty, which got on Julia's nerves.

"Leave everything alone!" She growled. "I can't rest with you in here."

Seeing the hurt in Maureen's eyes, I suggested we step outside. It wasn't like Julia to yell at her mother like that, but these were difficult times, which neither of them, so far as I knew, had formally acknowledged to each other. Standing in the hospital corridor, outside Julia's room, Maureen asked me about Bermuda. The door to Julia's room was open and we could see her lying on the bed, eyes closed in rest, as a nurse prepped a drug tray.

"Lloyd and I went there, let's see, was it nineteen-eighty-three?" She looked over at Lloyd, who had just finished questioning a hospital technician about the broken television in his daughter's room. He clearly didn't appreciate being made a part of our conversation.

"Eighty-four," he said gruffly.

"It's probably changed a lot since then. I remember the pink sand."

"The pink sand," I repeated. "And the blue water."

Not knowing what else to do, I carried on – the flowering hedges, the clean air, the night sky, the storm, the bobolinks – until it became apparent that the subject of Bermuda, which had meant to steer us clear of discomfort, was now the source of it.

"This must be a bit of a shock for you. We should have told you what was going on."

I once had a job as a waiter and, being young, I'd taken my customers' friendliness as an invitation to engage in conversa-tion. I remembered the way their faces tightened when they realized I wasn't going away. That was the face Maureen and Lloyd gave me now.

"Julia never gave us any trouble," Maureen said, glancing into her daughter's room, then turning away as if intimidated. In many ways Julia was a stranger to her, as was her husband who, without saying a word, had slipped away, probably to find out what could be done about the broken television.

Emily and Duncan were more like hospital patients than visiting guests – they belonged with the sick, the disturbed, and the medicated. Duncan especially. He spoke of the hepatitis he'd contracted while filming the commune in Arizona and, in sympathy with Julia's condition but more likely because of the stress he was under, appeared to be experiencing a relapse. I'd become conditioned to placing my father in specific locations – the office, The Steak House – and it was somewhat shocking to find him outside his setting – like an escaped zoo animal who'd ended up in someone's backyard. In contrast to Lloyd Riddell, who looked as if he'd been hired to run the hospital, Duncan gamely shuffled down the linoleum hallways, greeting fellow patients with an insider's nod. He would have loved a wheelchair, and a friendly nurse to push it.

Not comfortable with the subject of pregnancy, but for entirely different reasons than the Riddells, he sat down in the corner chair, which Maureen had correctly moved to the window, and stared out at the sky. Strange though it was, I suppressed an urge to hold his hand.

Emily lay on the bed with Julia. She wanted to know everything about Julia's personal, as opposed to medical, condition:

What was her pain like? When had it started? Was she sad? Or maybe angry? With Dr. Henderson? Her son? God?

My mother made herself hugely comfortable inside the room Maureen had so attentively decorated. I felt sorry for Maureen, who plainly was at a loss when faced with my mother's inquiries and Julia's animated responses. She and Lloyd were not stupid, nor were they mean, cold, or shallow; they just didn't know how to talk to Julia like my mother could.

The only Riddell capable of displacing my mother was Barry. He was Julia's favourite and sat by her bed for hours, only going downstairs when he knew Maureen was busy so he'd have free rein in the cafeteria. He'd been downstairs that morning but had returned, to everyone's surprise, with Christy. She wore the same summer hat I'd seen when we'd first met, but she plucked it off when she walked into the room. Barry took hold of Christy's wrist and lifted up her hand, displaying her five pudgy fingers that wiggled coquettishly before us. It was then we spotted the ring.

"We're married," Barry said.

Christy, too excited, jumped up and down, as if she were skipping a rope. "I love you." I assumed she meant all of us, not just Barry.

Maureen Riddell began to cry.

Which was awkward because no one knew if her tears were of joy, sorrow, or pent-up tension at having a daughter in the hospital. Lloyd's face reddened in fury, but with people in the room he tried to hold his temper.

"What do you mean you're married? Where did you get the money for a ring?"

The answer was obvious; he was just too angry to see it.

"I got it from making birds," said Barry.

Maureen's sobs grew louder.

"You think," said Lloyd, "that just because you move into an apartment and go to work at a job, both of which I'm paying for, that you can go off and get married without telling anyone?"

Again, the answer was obvious.

"I won't allow it!" yelled Lloyd, losing his restraint.

"They're already married, Dad," Julia quietly pointed out.

In all the commotion we'd forgotten her. She looked drained but striking in her pale, sleepy fatigue. She beckoned her family to come forward and they huddled around her as if she were a failing queen. My family was quiet for once, outsiders in someone else's family drama. Julia kissed her brother, then Christy. "I want to have a party for you and my new sister-in-law at our house." She turned to her mother. "And I want you to stop crying. And, Dad, go have a drink somewhere and calm down, it's not the end of the world. Barry deserves to be happy. Now I want everyone to go except Luke because I'm tired and need to get some rest."

A crisis highlights the proper, hierarchical order of relationships. Grieving parents, concerned in-laws, all are banished except the spouse who is like a trump card, overriding all others in the deck. The memory of Julia's interminable games of solitude in Bermuda came back to me, how she played card after card, hand after hand, patiently waiting her turn to win.

Now that our own drama had come to an end – and Julia had admitted it was the end, hadn't she? – I wanted to crawl in to bed beside her and fall asleep, but I remained standing, alert with deliberate sympathy.

"Barry and Christy's marriage is a bit of a surprise," I said, and I decided to explain the circumstances of Barry's employment. I confessed that the salary I'd paid her brother had actually come from Lloyd.

"So it was my father who paid for the ring?" Julia was delighted by the outcome. "Serves him right."

"I guess I wasn't a very good spy for your father. But I liked Christy and my mind was on other things."

"Speaking of which . . ."

Julia rolled slightly to her side and pulled out from beneath her body a manila envelope, which she then handed to me.

"What's this?"

"I don't want you to open it right now. Take it home and when you're feeling calm – maybe you should join my father and have a drink – I want you to sit down, take a breath, then read what's inside and think very carefully about what I'm asking you to do."

I recalled that as I was saying goodbye to the Riddells, thinking to myself how clueless they'd been about their children, I'd caught sight of Emily leaning over my wife's bed and handing her something. It must have been this envelope. I walked down the corridor, past the nursing stations illuminated like ships at sea, the muffled moans of patients sounding like shipwrecked survivors, and tore off the seal. To my credit, I didn't scream when I saw what was inside, because I was in a very public place, filled with sick people. My mother was waiting for me at the end of the hallway, and I stormed over to her, waving the papers in her face.

"How could you do this to me? Your own son!"

"What I did is solve your problems. Somebody has to make the hard decisions."

Directly behind my mother was a door that said, Warning, Hazardous Material, Do Not Enter. *One push*, I thought, *just one push and she'd be gone*.

"Where's Dad?" I said. "What does he think of this?"

"Your father's gone home."

*Of course he had.*

"He never has to deal with anything, does he?" I said bitterly. "He just gets to run and hide and let everyone else take care of the mess."

"Remind you of someone? Luke, you hide away from the world for fear it will ask something of you. Julia has suffered. I've suffered. You can help make things right. Just sign the papers."

"I'll never do it," I said. "Ever."

I arrived at the factory to find Philip sitting in my office chair with Tamara on his lap. The screen saver on the new computer Roger had set up showed a picture of them, plus Tamara's two children, wearing conical birthday hats. I felt awkward and out of place.

"Sorry to interrupt," I said. It was the first time I'd seen Tamara since returning from Bermuda.

"You're not interrupting." Tamara smiled, and I knew, at that precise moment, that we didn't like each other. I also knew I had nothing to fear from her. She'd already forgotten all about me. She clasped her arms around Philip's neck, taking possession of him. "I've made some coffee."

"Uh, thanks."

The three of us spoke cautiously of work. I no longer knew much of what was going on, what supplies we needed, how many birds were on order, or how many we'd made. Philip filled me in on the details and I found, as always, that he'd done a very good job.

"Tamara's been working extra hours," he said.

"Sure, that's fine."

"We needed the extra hands."

Later that morning I stepped into a pair of Hans's overalls, pulled a mask over my face, and dipped bird parts into vats of white paint, pegging each dripping limb to the clothesline until it sagged with the weight. I went outside for some fresh air, imagining how many birds I'd made since my days in the basement and how long all the clotheslines would be if I strung them end to end. I was sick of birds. They sweated paint and smelled of sawdust and there were times when I thought I'd never dislodge their sour odour from my nostrils. Mr. Chang walked out of his warehouse, as always a clipboard in hand, to examine another shipment of lamps. The door behind him opened; his wife, I thought.

It was Hans.

"I never knew how miserable I looked," he said, because I was wearing his painting overalls and because I was, without a doubt, unhappy. Hans wore grey flannel pants, a well-cut blue shirt, and sported a watch on his wrist that he may or may not have always worn but I'd never noticed before. The effect was even more startling than seeing him walk out of the Changs' warehouse; he was like a freed man who'd been given back his clothes after a long incarceration. Men in prison don't wear watches.

"Look," he said, pointing to the lampshades.

Not noticing anything at first, my eyes wandered back to Hans. But I looked again and, just as I'd finally noticed the bobolinks, I picked out the small birds painted on the lampshades.

"I designed them specially for the Changs."

"Limited edition," said Mr. Chang proudly, thumping Hans on the back.

I wordlessly accepted Hans's invitation to follow him across the car park, the cuffs of my overalls scraping the asphalt. We were going to his studio, which I'd only been to once before, when he'd first started working for me. He had always been my neighbour, and yet when he'd walked out the doors of the bird factory, it was as if he had stepped into a parallel universe.

Hans pulled out a set of keys.

"I want to show you something."

Fiddling with the lock, Hans opened his door and for a moment I thought there'd been a mistake.

"I don't understand," I said.

"Yes you do. It was why I was fired."

The only light came from the open front door, but Hans kept away from the light switch; it wasn't so much that my eyes needed to adjust, but my mind.

"It's the bird factory," I whispered.

More precisely, it was the painting room, from which I'd just come from and for which I was still dressed, and as I stepped inside in astonishment, I saw the rows of birds, the paint pans, the clotheslines. Only it wasn't birds hanging from the pins, but human body parts, hands and feet and thighs, fingers too, and thick, fat toes.

"It's like a nightmare."

"Yes."

"And you sleep here?"

"Yes."

"And that was why you were taking material from the bird factory, so you could build this?"

"Until Lurch caught me. But it was okay, because I was almost finished my work for the gallery."

"What gallery?"

"The Mississauga Centre for the Arts."

"I didn't know Mississauga *had* a Centre for the Arts."

"There's more to Mississauga than birds and lampshades."

Hans led me deeper into the room and when we reached the back corner, next to his cot, I spotted stacks of bird wings, of all shapes and sizes, rising up from the floor.

"I will lay all the wings on the ground, like dead animals. I will ask people to step on them."

"From what I can see, I'm the one you want to step on."

"I think you step on yourself. I saw you with Tamara."

"When?"

"When it mattered. I had come in to take more materials for my installation. But I saw you."

"Nothing happened," I said, lowering my head.

"Everything happened."

I saw his point.

"It's been difficult." And then all at once I told Hans about Julia, about how sick she'd been and how we'd tried to have a baby, about the storm and the bobolinks, lying exhausted on the ground. I told him everything in that dim, strange room of his.

Finally, when I'd finished talking, Hans said, "You know, I've learned from working at the bird factory that you should take what is bad and never pretend that it is any better. Then you will be okay."

Afterwards, getting into my car for the drive to the hospital, I picked up the manila envelope from the dashboard and signed the adoption papers for Rosemary and Duncan's baby.

# How It Begins

ADAM IS IN MY ARMS, kicking his legs in hunger. He wants food. He always wants food and, against all my expectations, I always want to give it to him. He can't be breastfed, of course, so we use formula. I like cooking it up, pouring the hot milk into its plastic containers, feeling it slowly cool in my hands.

Barry and Christy, Lloyd and Maureen – the Riddell clan of which I am a part – are getting ready to leave. Barry, for his wedding party, is wearing a houndstooth jacket Julia purchased for him, because he's always wanted to wear a houndstooth jacket and since it is his wedding party, he can wear what he wants.

Christy is still admiring the ring on her finger – something I've seen her doing all afternoon – and she holds it up for Adam's inspection, but Adam wants food not rings and I take him to the kitchen.

I don't pretend Adam just dropped into my arms one sunny afternoon – I signed papers, and saw a lawyer, and answered questions from government-appointed social workers, who visited our house to certify our fitness to become parents – but, in point of fact, Adam *was* just dropped into my arms one sunny afternoon. Julia brought him up the front steps and held him out to me. "Your son," she said.

Duncan is in the kitchen, alone. He says nothing, just stares quizzically at Adam. He's drunk, though that's to be expected.

"Do you want to feed him?" I ask, picking up a baby bottle.

Duncan shakes his head and turns to pour himself another rum and Coke. He swirls the rum with his index finger, while I pop the plastic nipple into Adam's mouth. I watch Adam drink, then my father.

He's never held Adam in his arms, at least not in front of me. I suppose in time he will become more used to what has happened, more familiar with the terms. I don't think we will ever talk about it. Strangely enough, I don't think we will ever need to. Adam is here. That's all. That's it.

Back in the living room, the Riddells are carting off the wedding presents, including the king-sized duvet and matching cotton covers printed with birds, a gift from Julia and me. Barry continues to work part-time at the factory, with half his wages covered by his father. He has learned how to take the bus to Mississauga. I don't go out there myself any more. Because of Roger, I can keep track of sales and inventory from a computer on the desk I've placed in the hall outside Adam's room. The work I do is very unnecessary and most of the time I use it as an excuse to be next to Adam. Philip and Tamara are slowly buying ownership in the business. It is my hope that they will buy me out completely in a few years.

Finished with his milk, Adam reaches out for his mother. Julia takes him from my arms and settles him on her shoulder, rubbing his back.

"He's tired," Julia says. "Let's put him to bed."

We walk upstairs and prepare Adam for bedtime. Everyone follows to wish him goodnight as we tuck him into his crib. Dangling overhead is a bobolink – a gift from Hans – with Adam's name printed in glow-in-the dark paint. At night, when I putter to the bathroom, I see it there, glowing: ADAM.

In the soft hush of the nursery, as we all gather around, I take Julia's hand. It occurs to me that Hans is wrong. Julia has never accepted bad things and that is why she has been able to make them better.

Everyone is quiet for a moment until my mother, who always has to have the final word, says, "Well, I guess birds of a feather stick together."

And, incredibly, we all start laughing.

## Acknowledgements

Many thanks to Sean Franey and Jocelyn Smith for information, Rosemary Sullivan for good luck, Eithne and Michael Goddard for food and advice, and Ellen Seligman for her support. Finally, my thanks to Jennifer Lambert, whose time, dedication, and editorial acumen are deeply appreciated.